# Praise for Gail Scott

"Gail Scott moves through the ghost world she calls Paris
with grace and intelligence in this troubling and poignant
book of shadows and their elaborations."
—Carole Maso—

"*My Paris* is a tour de force of technique, style, and soul."
—Brad Hooper, *Booklist* (starred review)—

"In *Heroine* . . . the city of Montréal comes into a focus
as precise and vivid as *Mrs. Dalloway*'s London."
—*Village Voice*—

"Gail Scott is one of the most gutsy writers around."
—*Toronto Globe and Mail*—

"Part novel, part essay, part travel diary, part memoir,
part dialogue, part prose poem, *My Paris* is a
pointillistic tour de force."
—Charles Bernstein—

# Other Books by Gail Scott

NOVELS

Heroine
Main Brides

SHORT STORIES

Spare Parts Plus Two

ESSAYS

Spaces Like Stairs
La théorie, un dimanche (with Nicole Brossard et al.)

# MY PARIS

# GAIL SCOTT

Dalkey Archive Press

Library of Congress Cataloging-in-Publication Data

Scott, Gail, 1945–
    My Paris / Gail Scott.— 1st Dalkey Archive ed.
        p. cm.
    ISBN 1-56478-297-2 (acid-free paper)
    1. Canadians—France—Fiction. 2. Women—France—Fiction. 3. Paris
    (France)—Fiction. I. Title.

    PR9199.3.S35M9 2003
    813'.54—dc22

                                                            2003055447

Partially funded by grants from the Lannan Foundation and the Illinois Arts Council,
a state agency.

Dalkey Archive Press books are published by the Center for Book Culture, a nonprofit
organization.

www.centerforbookculture.org

Narrator on author: She kept an old postcard of a white Saltimbanque stuck on the fridge. Titled "Man in experiment, white-clad and sunlit, passing black screen on a curved white sidewalk." Giving an odd feeling of running in reverse while trying to grasp a point in the future she didn't want to think about. These pages are from that faux-deco studio she won in the lottery. Plus (probably) the New Year's Eve trip she inveigled Y into paying for. The time she thought she saw her Saltimbanque in the Luxembourg. Dancing along a pathetic low railing. Inches off the ground. Balancing as if on a highwire tightrope. Toeing to the left. To the right. Bowing to the audience (no one was watching). He seemed a white-painted clown. Possibly from "the south." Or else a scared nomad. With nowhere to go.

1. LIKE A HEROINE FROM BALZAC. I AM ON A DIVAN. NARROW. COVERED with a small abstract black-and-white print. At end a rice-paper screen. Three mahogany-framed partitions. Pale eggshell walls curving gracefully at corners. Staring up at slender almost ceiling-high radiators. A library with four crescent shelves. Low comfortable black-and-white canapé. Low end tables. Glass posed on metal. Grey round dining table and matching chairs on heavy chrome legs. Teak desk with computer. Teak console with television. Video. Fax. Green and yellow rugs on hardwood floors. One with designer's initials in the corner.

This isn't what I expected. I feel a little strange (guilty). In this elegance. Bathed by the white light coming through the white transparent curtains. Outside the treed boulevard. Traffic racing up and down making such a din. My nemesis. For being here. Sitting with my earplugs. Music turned up high. Still I hear the racket.

2. Now on canapé near window. Listening to some radio station. Not Ferrat singing Aragon. Nor Satie nor Barbara. The new France. Conjuring up mint in the margins. Rosewater. Orange. Sweet nutcakes of the medinas of Morocco. Looking out at chic boulevard Raspail. At the smartly dressed women airing tiny dogs on the boulevard strip down the middle. Siding with the Arab music. Though careful not to turn it up too loud. For fear of arousing the suspicions of the neighbour.

A duchess—saying the moustached man. Sent to fetch me at the airport. Depositing me at my door. See her husband climbing up the stairs carrying a statue. What suspicions. True I don't have

7

the proper papers. Too late to the consulate for a visa. Permitting me to stay. Now it takes six weeks where it used to take an hour. The Right having come to power. Cops everywhere in the neighbourhood. A block away they're posted beside a rather nice café. I refuse to go there. S saying I'm ridiculous. Failing to mention the new strictness regarding visas. Will normalement be applied selectively. To people from "the south." I.e. Africa. Maghrebia.

3. Rain. Earlier cranked up the varnished horizontal wood-slat outer blind or "store." With the ivory handle hidden behind the curtains. People straight as pokers at the bus stop below. Or rushing carrying baguettes. Hair slick and neat in straight lines from the nape to the cheek. Some leaning forward. To examine suits in windows of exclusive men's shop. Across street. Then lying back on divan by rice-paper screen. By roxy-painted night-table. With Walter Benjamin's 1000-page volume—*Paris, Capitale du XIX$^e$ siècle*—on it. Left by previous studio occupant. Cover photo of ornate decorative balcony. Topped by mirror reflecting the glass-and-iron ceiling of one of those labyrinthine 19th-century passages or arcades. They used to forge through buildings. The labyrinth the shape of ancient utopias.

Like a snail saying the little moustached man. Driving in from the airport. As we leaving periphery. Entering curved streets of enclave. Grey six-or-seven-storey buildings against oyster sky. Wrought-iron railings. Shutters. Little crooked parks. Over there somewhere that quiet modest quarter. The whitewashed artist's studio. Seen in the movies.

Of course I'm glad to be here.

4. Walk with S along a curved white street. Rue de Varenne or rue du Bac. Hot and sunny. Stark shadows cast by walls of 18th-century buildings. Small French cars parked half on sidewalk. Two cops by the café. Le ministère est par là, the ministry's over there. S saying with shrug. A veteran of May '68. And subsequent productions. Knowing when to regard them. As furniture.

This walk starting with me looking out window. Seeing S on opposite corner. Smoking. Preoccupied. Instead of rushing over. Like she doing. When visiting chez nous. Reinforcing sense I not at all in Paris I expecting. Having imagined things less glossy. More comfily dilapidated. As in HÔTEL SPHINX where Nadja used to live. Or old shops. Teeming with "marvellous" detritus. Such as Breton's strange curved spoon with tiny woman's heel holding up the handle. Or that ornate dovecote. With ledge round top. To keep birdshit from falling on your head. Somewhere in countryside.

In polished faubourg Saint-Germain nothing left to chance.

S crossing over. Loudly rattling the heavy wrought-iron door. To see if it locked. I am mortified. The concierge tearing from her little mahogany loge. With its lace and pink satin curtains. Taking in S's overly casual dress. Loose T-shirt. Loose black jeans. Heavy grey knapsack laden down with books. A laid-back look being in just now. Thank god. Women even wearing sneakers. Italian leather-lined. Plus the knapsack must be black. Carried nonchalantly off one shoulder. As fake nonchalant as a Catherine Deneuve movie.

On the hot street I do see one woman appearing to be mad. Shuffling painfully along. Staring at us from pupils that have almost disappeared under lids. But her haircut short and straight. Bangs to brow. Very neat. Veston buttoned up despite heat. Cheap runners clean. We crossing from haughty 7th. To less haughty 6th. Walking down Vieux-Colombier, Old Dovecote Street. More shiny shops. Choked right now with tourists. Emerging on place Saint-Sulpice. With asymmetrical church. Fountain. Pigeons. Henry Miller full of being American finding the belfries too fat. The incense too smelly. The pigeons too mellifluous.

Realism—the view of One.

5. What is it about Paris. Trying to see past sleepless nights from traffic. Choking on pollution. Overly self-conscious of appearance. Hair neat and smooth. Shiny shoes. Then one day noticing standing automatically straighter. The way Parisians do. Noticing the earthy naughty odours of a hundred different cheeses. Wafting

entwined from a cheese shop. One alive and oozing through its wax paper in her bag. Plus a lambchop so pink she could kiss it. Nice olives. Smiling she enters the lobby of her building. This nourishment of senses conferring on her. A surface more shiny—

Maybe already less a traveller. Than a sort of flâneur (of interior!). Though Benjamin saying flâneur already hawking observations. Like simple journalist. By time of Baudelaire. Anyway sitting on canapé. Looking out window. Rain streaking pane. Not having found dream café yet. Probably having to leave faubourg. In this manner whiling away the dangerous snare of late afternoon. Manufacturing alcoholics. Until it's late when slipping off cushion. Showering. Dressing. Corning up with calf-length tights. Short flowered skirt. Black top. Rushing down Raspail. Choosing café near more ordinary 6th. Growing crowded. Workers drinking beer or wine. At bar. Pulling wallets from belts. At smalls of their backs. Elegant women with pretty shopping bags. Ordering non-alcoholic drinks. Grenadine. Or mint. For the skin.

Glazed look of waiter. Saying outfit doesn't pass. Unless it's my anglo-québécois accent. Putting that sheen on his face. In paling light people rushing by. Woman nibbling a baguette. Protruding from a grocery bag. Another biting into large chocolate bar. Métro-boulot-dodo. I opening *Nadja*. Loving how Breton displacing question "who am I?" Onto old French adage. Whom do I haunt?

Bus with large image of Bambi. Going by window.

6. The marvellous *is* to be had. I thinking at 5:30a. Looking out window. Pale blue sky beyond anarchy of chimney pots. You just have to pierce the smugness of the surface. Below on sidewalk the pale man. Living in basement. To exit—daily skirting edge of lobby's pale-green artfully rough-cut marble tiles. Laid on diagonal. Past mahogany cage elevator. Probably a collector's item. Concierge's loge on left. Only slightly larger. Over this my studio. Plus grand suite of duchess. Over us likely that rich Senegalese family. On top of them—young film-industry woman. Very French cheekbones. Chin dimple. I meeting on stairs.

But exhausted. So late again when slipping off cushion. Clearly not flâneur. In later 19th-century sense of industriously strolling. I.e. practically an A-type personality. According to Benjamin. Whose round glasses. Susceptible physiognomy. On photo. Found in drawer of black inlaid TV/fax/video console. Resembling friend R's from Winnipeg. Whereas I preferring to lie back in interior of peluche. Though dressing more quickly now to pass. Shoes shined. Hair crimped. Pants pressed. Also by skipping lunch. Leaving studio slightly messy. Having more time to wander. Racing towards Saint-Germain. Red jeans and Beatles's-style polka-dot jacket. Through Quartier Latin. Dodging Germans. Scandinavians. Americans. Thinking how French wanting to be rid of foreigners. *Some* foreigners. S saying. Leaves along street turning up little gold sequins in the setting sun. Only real example of true Parisian chic. Magnificent African-French woman in calf-length fitted dress. Platform heels. Hair twisted in two plaits over little ears.

Left into café LE CLUNY. As lasse, dazed. From fatigue. As day of arrival. Being décalée, time-gapped. As French calling jet-lagged. Anyway running. Because meeting other writers from French-speaking America. Likewise occupying studios. Won in arts' competitions. Your accent's lovely saying one. Meaning not authentic. (Mother being English.) Measuring my heavy diphthongs. Against her rhythmic québécois phonemes. Parisians looking down on. Tu vas faire de si belles conquêtes, people will be charmed.

You'd have lost it if you wanted—saying another.

A third putting her hand on my shoulder. Crossing pont Marie to île Saint-Louis. We pausing to watch sunset. Little gold-tipped brown ripples. Endlessly reproduced in cinema. Brown light seeping up between leafy banks of Seine. C busy incanting various crêpe *farces*. Oeuf/tomate. Bacon/oeuf/fromage/ratatouille. Boudin/pomme. Roquefort/noix. Gallic profile leaning. Full lips smiling. Pleasure!

Does one have the right. It occurring to me this maybe a Protestant way of thinking.

I asking her if her mother would be jealous.

11

7. Today a bright baby-blue sky delineates black roofs and sky-line. Popping bubbles in the air. Or—nothing delineates the sky-line. Disorder of roof gardens. Fancy little huts built up there on sly. Barely visible from boulevard. Sloping in ordered lines of green-framed windows. Neat rows of awnings. Straight and stiff. Wrought-iron fence—symmetry of spears with little points on top. Geometric patterns on grilles bordering casement windows. Wondering how much of French mania for detail. Seeping into brain.

The doorbell rings. Worker with huge drill entering. Walking across floor. Bending grey head and starting to drill large hole. Through eggshell plaster. Through layer of brick. Then stone. For a ventilator he saying. Vibrations. Unbelievable racket. Doorbell ringing again. The concierge. Hand on her heart. Having been to sixth floor and back. Trying to find the noise. I imagining layers of women with crossed stockinged legs. Pumps. Tailored skirts. Drinking tea on canapés. In a Nathalie Sarraute novel. Chatting chatting. Comme si de rien n'était, as if nothing happening.

The duchess's in the country.

The sky—so blue suddenly turning grey. The workman bent over showing the top of a diaper. Unless it's his wallet. Drilling very slowly. And I wanting to go out. Crossing to the right bank. To one of those beautiful old commercial passages or arcades. B calling miniatures. Of 19th-century Paris. Doorbell once more. Concierge again. As pleased as a cat. Beside her man with abbreviated legs. Large barrel chest. Finest linen shirt I've ever seen. Shined-back black hair. Snapping eyes. Incompétent he screaming. At worker. Claiming growing cracks in ceiling of his boutique. Directly below. Selling line of androgynous under- and casual-wear. This could be trouble. Will the cops come. Will they hear my accent and ask to see my passport.

It turning out to be theatre. Walking up Raspail. Towards closest noisy café. Pleased to have grasped this. Shining boots. Pressed pants. Carrying *Le Monde*. Nice young waiter. Hair cut short on sides and long in the back. As if still in '70s. Talking to biker on terrasse. Otherwise—after-work crowd. Hands coming out of well-pressed sleeves. Holding cigarettes or energetically motioning. Though likely exhausted. The body capable of gestures prompting understanding. Contrary to indication. Traffic honking and screeching. By open French doors.

8. Raining. Cats. Therefore returning to divan. Lying back on finest black-and-white sheets. To point of silky. Like Balzac's *Girl with Golden Eyes*. Naturellement no marquise. Keeping "one" sequestered. For sake of love. With old duenna, servant. Bringing fresh bread. Rich delicate butter. Picked by chance from fromagerie's ten sorts. Jam. Coffee. Anyway—returning to divan. And lifting heavy volume of B's *Paris, Capitale du XIX^e*. From turquoise roxy-painted bedside table. Subtitle *Le livre des passages*. *Passagenwerk* in German. Not yet available in English. Therefore weighing the more delightfully on wrists. Not a real history. Rather—vast collection of 19th-century quotes and anecdotes. Initially seeming huge pile of detritus. But—on looking closer. More like montage. Possibly assembled using old surrealist trick. Of free association. I opening at contents' list. "A"—*Passages*—glass-roofed arcades, malls. Hawking 19th century's new imperial luxury. Juxtaposed on "B"— *Mode*. Each new season. Ironizing time. Next to "C"—*Antique Paris, catacombes, démolitions*—Paris's underpinnings. Pointing to "D"—*L'ennui*—Eternal return. Present tense of dandy. Hovering over "E"—*Haussmannisation, combats des barricades*— Haussmann's wide boulevards. Versus the people. Progress's double coin. Segueing into "J"—Poet *Baudelaire*. First modern. Peer of "M"—*Flâneur*—whose initial post-French-Revolutionary languor not ultimately resisting rising capitalist market. "X/Y"—*Marx*— realism. Next to *Photography . . . Social movements. Dolls. Automatons.*

A person could wander here for months.

9. Last night took S to mediaeval music concert. In old thermal baths at HÔTEL DE CLUNY. Someone gave me tickets. Walking along rue de Grenelle she saying I seem mal foutue, badly shoed. In my

cowboy boots. Actually I trailing to look at boutiques. Composed of mannequins singing praises to the highest peons of the mode. Kenzo. Yves St. Laurent. And I forget who. As rhythmic as the news is how B describing la mode. Appearance of every new edition raising spectre of caesura. Ironic antidote to perpetual melancholy. Which melancholy surfacing in vaulted room of old thermal baths. Group of young people from all points of globe. In brightly coloured gauze. Singing high songs from early in millennium. Mostly religious. Their fresh voices bouncing off thick sandbrick walls. Echoing in empty pool. With lions' heads on corners. One song a very humorous quick Latin equivalent of two-step. About death.

10. Today might try and find one of those old 19th-century passages. B likening to ghost stepping right through city blocks. They're *everywhere* S saying. Curved arm gesturing. To the left bank. To the right. Brown eyes ironic. Regarding my desire. For her beloved Paris. Where she has hidden. Thrown pavés, paving stones. Been a city worker. Fine profile turning this way or that. Always seeking new streets to step down. As if a walk were a caress.

But passages not streets. The peculiar light of their aging glass-and-iron roofs. In prime conferring lineage of greenhouse. Replete with palms. Parrots. Mirrors. Moist alleys of desire. Kind of *locus classicus* of B's strange Paris history. I now consuming daily. Lying back on divan. With fresh bread from bakery. Coffee. After raising outer store or shutter. And looking down on traffic. Volume earlier falling open. At allusion to favourite Balzac heroine: *Girl with Golden Eyes.* In some oriental get-up. Guarded by duenna. In absence of marquise. So girl incapable of making contact with handsome young Tom. Who stalking her in Tuileries. Before marquise finding out. And killing her. Allusion not far from anecdote about ancient Chinese puzzle. Representing hachured parts of human form. Prefiguring cubism. Which puzzle fashionable under Second Empire. Reign of terror and indifference. According to B.

The marquise's a very jealous lover.

And S's avoiding me. As if Paris light unflattering. Intimating I spoiled. Studio grant a leisure lottery. Therefore not arranging meeting with left-bank friends. In Montparnasse café. Gay editor. Going blind from AIDS. Spicy Bretonne. Writing about seduction. In Paris urinals. German anarchist. Plus lipstick dyke from suburbs. Smiling mockingly.

11. Walking yesterday. Down rue du Bac, Embarkment Street. Across pont Royal. Through jardin des Tuileries. Paris's heart and best defence. Why defence. Because a garden. Therefore beautiful. Or defence of Cartesian way of thinking. Long straight alleys. Geometric flowers. Copses symmetrical. Every detail. Gesture. Thought out infinitesimally. Where the *Girl with Golden Eyes*. While taking constitutional. First laying eyes on Tom. Who greatly turning her on. Heading down grand central alley. Dramatically in line with giant courtyards of Louvre. And distant Champs-Élysées. Blocks of prime real estate. Stretching green along river. So much formal public space. Seeming impossible. Under late capitalism.

It also engulfing late-20th stroller. Breathing in pollution. Crossing another traffic-choked avenue. In search of one of those passages. B calling galleries of desire. Confusing rue Croix-des-Petits-Champs/Cross-of-Little-Fields Street. With rue des Petits-Champs/Little Fields Street. As if in the country. Passing and repassing. Several armed gendarmes. Patrolling Banque de France. Making wide berth. Down other side of street. Fortunately stumbling on galérie VERO-DODAT. *VE-RO DO-DAT.* What pleasure in a name! After two butchers. Ionian-style columns. Holding up entrance. Repeated down corridor in vertical geometrical motif. Mahogany and brass separating shop windows.

She stepping in. Fortunately or unfortunately. Unstalked by anyone. Walking quickly over marble floor. Under dim painted panels. Gold-leaf trimmed ceilings. Under pigeons nesting. In glass-and-iron roof. Place completely empty. No one drinking coffee. No one buying lingerie. In thinly stocked boutique. One African-French woman polishing brass trim. On mahogany boutique front. Quickly she stepping. Past old doll shop. Past luthier, stringed-instrument maker. Statues. Leather furniture. Old bound books. And back. Forgetting even to check if famous GASTRONOMIE COSMOPOLITE sign. Still existing. With lettering of intertwined fish. Chicken. Livers. Down corner café stairs to pissoir. Noticing through door opposite cubicle. Woman in little black dress. Pushing hefty wine barrel. Along stone-paved underground street.

And up onto boulevards. Still hurrying. Past epoch's current galleries of desire. Chic small boutiques. Suffering capital's latest conspiracy. Globalization. So windows along Saint-Germain. Screaming SOLDES, SALES of exquisite French teal-blue suede sofas. Brightly coloured Kenzo silk prints. Curved lamps. Posturing this way and that. As if about to do the tango. Women's boots with little stud metal designs at the ankle. Screaming ESCOMPTES. RABAIS. RÉDUCTIONS. Same panic repeated nightly on TV. Fluctuating franc. Endless company layoffs.

At apogée of passages it fashionable to walk. Leading a tortoise.


12. S at last calling. We meeting in café with bird's-eye tabletops. Pseudo art-nouveau lightshades. Practically on traffic island. Drowning conversation. Still it feeling so good. Drinking cool Beaujolais. Smoking Gauloises légères. Trying to draw her to me. Saying I considering little book. On murdered women wanderers. Albeit so far theoretical (lacking anecdotes). She shrugging. Art Equals Commerce. Plus que jamais, more than ever. Is this an objective analysis. Impeccable in its materialism. Or statement of principle. I saying nothing. If art equals commerce. There is no artist. On returning to apartment—seeing refrigerator not exchanged. For one with glaçons, ice cubes. As arranged with previous studio occupant. Not giving damn about glaçons. But walking around feeling abandoned. Paranoid. Persona non grata.

To charm requiring anecdotes.

Below on boulevard—green-clad worker from "south." Vacuuming up dog shit. Followed by other green-clad guy. Green broom and matching refuse bag. Against backdrop of that fine men's store opposite. Windows of exquisitely stitched collars. Reflecting meridian strip. Where Gertrude Stein's poodle Basket used to shit. With other rich expatriate puppies. Thinking Paris belonging to them. Turn on some Arab music. Low.

In a modest neighbourhood—surely more anecdotes. Though perhaps the faubourg. With all its perfect people. *Suiting* this period. This mood.

On TV: gardening show. In Sarajevo. Women squatting. Ducking snipers.

13. Went and sat in café on boulevard des Sèvres for a few minutes at dusk. Watching the night hawks flitting among white chimneys. Leaving again. A faded day. Lack of sleep. Too much time spent eating. Dressing.

Young woman sitting down beside me. In rue de Babylone café earlier. Long black hair against white Parisian skin. Some kind of spotless white culottes. Blue tunic over. Perfect nails. Perfectly smooth legs. Snow-white sandals. Emitting an odour evoking sublime cleanliness. Faintly lemon. Appreciating her as much as waiter.

But bored. Sick of traffic. Of having Barclay's Bank. For neighbour.

14. Now happy. Sitting in jardin des Luxembourg. Having walked several blocks beyond usual noisy Sèvres-Babylone café. Air green. Magnificent. Sun shining through dappled leaves. On terrasse by little round chalet with lots of windows. Painted green. Little girls with sailor hats and starched striped dresses. Redhaired mother and redhaired daughter. Chatting amicably. Group of adolescent males. Ce n'est pas vrai says one. Parce que tu n'as pas dit que tu as vu la Vierge, it's not true because you didn't swear on the Virgin. Two leather-clad junkies. Disappearing down cement stairs of

17

pissoir. Girl with blue bow sitting on chair. Feet high above ground. Sipping from straw. Reading book called *Célia*. Already perfect lady. Or already aware what's expected of her. Crook in her finger. Down little set of stairs—junkies closing in on round lady washroom attendant. Fingering her saucer of tips. To charm requiring anecdotes. I lolling above. In ambience of impressionist painting. Juxtaposed on something darker. Under.

The 20th century was only young at its beginning. Gertrude Stein saying. She then abolishing commas.

15. Last night looking out at—taking wild guess—Second Empire building. On corner. No. Likely slightly later: post-Commune. With flagrant stuck-on cement floral decoration. Swags. Bows. Bouquets. Such bogus use of robust new construction materials. B saying. Representing lowest point in architecture. Corresponding to period of greatest political depression. Following Commune defeat of 1871.

Anyway I staring. At alternate round and square bay windows. Each cased in different foliage. Wondering if all ends of centuries similar. When—in one of those coincidences of seeing— beautiful woman suddenly appearing. On balcony. True Parisian of neighbourhood. Each blonde strand combed and pinned back. Fairly short décolletée black dress. Balcony door wide open. Room behind painted white. Almost smelling her perfume. Just now checking again. French doors still open. White shirred Italian-style curtains. Half-mast. Round plant looking green and healthy. Behind low iron railing. Similar to railing across bottom of my studio casement windows. Supposedly keeping people from falling. Off narrow ledge. Instead of floral—mine a diamond pattern. Art deco—previous studio occupant saying.

But. Morning. Slightly grey. Rainy. Her shutters still drawn. I noticing. Peeking through wooden laths of outer blind or store. Without raising. If raised—concierge taking as signal I up. Therefore bringing mail. Meaning dressing. Showering. Tidying. Before she ringing bell. Instead making coffee in pénombre. Coffee-maker beeping electronically. Slicing odorous pain de campagne, country bread. Bought the night before. Slapping on thick layers of butter. Turning on *France-Culture*. Very smooth accents. Returning to bed. With B. Who saying passages. With their light coming from above. Elegant façades. A world unto themselves. Cities in miniature. Sets. Brusquely transforming with advent of boulevards. From luxury commerce. To alleyways of gambling. Prostitution. Perversely harbingered by names of old boutiques. LA FILLE D'HONNEUR, Maid of Honour. LA VESTALE, Vestal Virgin. LE PAGE INCONSTANT, Unfaithful Page. LE MASQUE DE FER, The Iron Mask. LE PETIT CHAPERON, Little Red Riding Hood. LA PETITE NANETTE, Little Nanette. AU COIN DE LA RUE, On the Corner.

16. In bed with grippe. Reading Simenon. Imagining street below as quiet village square. Not to hear traffic. Sleeping less in three weeks here. Than in one chez nous. 5:30a. Waking. Métro rumbling under. Conjuring half-wakening fever-damp corridors. Tepid pools of sewers. Subterranean passages. Whole underground that was other city. Of 19th-century unconscious. Ghosts seeing it as grid. Vertically from six- or seven-storey rooftops. Down through caves à vin. Métro tunnels. Catacombs. Dark large lake. Under fabulous masked Second Empire Opéra. Where Leroux's opera phantom hid.

Yesterday somnambulently crossing boulevard. Jarred to senses. By group of sleek black-clad motorcyclists bearing down on me. I leaping back on meridian strip. Eliciting proud grimace. From lead phallus. Watching them pass very straight. Clad in spotless leather. Helmets. High boots. Thinking: bikers. But too neat for that. Black armbands around sleeves: fascists. S poohpoohing this. More likely garde-de-corps for some high official.

Anyway mid-July in Paris. And I wrapped in blankets with my grippe carabinée, rifling cold. To use a term from chez nous. Oh don't say *carabinée* on phone. A young compatriot telling me. Certain words triggering automatic wiretap. What words—I asking quickly. B-o-m-b-e. P spelling out playfully. At other end of line. Near place de la Bastille. Quartier grouillant de vie, full of real people. Bof, pooh—rejoining S. Phones in your country tapped more than you think.

On the boulevard strip the ragged maples blow.

17. Sitting in café at Sèvres/Babylone. I.e. corner of Exquisite China/ Pursuit of Sensuous Pleasure. Homeless guy selling *Macadam, Pavement*. By métro. Thinking time to start wandering. From present bifurcation. Toward Hermit's Well. Stone's throw from Buffoon Street. Down Beaujolais Alley. Through Wolf's Crack or Breach. Hot Cat Road. Passage of Desire. Magenta Boulevard. Where walking Nadja towards HÔTEL SPHINX. Little Girls' Impasse. Saint Jacques' Ditch. B saying "one's" perception of Paris streets. Based on sensuality of names. Adding *we* (sic) never having felt sharpness of pavement stones. Under bare feet. *We* never having to check uneven flagstones. To see if suitable for bed.

Ordering espresso. Waiting for S. She having offered to help "program" electronic TV. Currently only capturing Belmondo types. Cigarettes in lips. Playing slot machines against white metal walls. Not the Paris I expecting. Waiting. I noticing a carved heart. With fish in middle. I.e. in place of heart's heart. On huge treetrunk bordering terrasse. Subtext maybe being A COLD FISH. Except cold fish in French. Meaning what it is. *A plate of cold fish*. Not cold heart. As in English. Two well-preserved elderly women now entering. Conjuring Léa and Charlotte. Courtesans from Colette. Class of women famous. For pragmatism in managing money. Never sentimental. Though Léa finally falling. For young boy she's taken on. One possibly in drag. Short curly hair. Cigarette between nice pink lips. Tailored coat. Gorgeous legs. In little pumps. The other with mass of bleached curls. Black tailored suit. Asking for aspirins.

Traffic roaring around.

If S not coming soon. Grippe will be worse. With draft. Brown tobacco smoke. Two gendarmes in front of BANQUE DE FRANCE. Across corner. I needing to change money. What if they asking to

20

see visa. Looking out studio window earlier. Two cops in different than usual uniform. Getting on bus. Checking passports—I saying. To S. When she finally arriving. Her brown eyes mocking. More likely employees of transport company. Checking people have punched their tickets. But why so many kinds of uniforms. What an army. Defending republic. Even Americans living here for years. Taking roundabout public transportation routes. Since new visa regulations. S saying this hysterical. Of course if *African*-American . . . I saying we can't sit here for coffee. Because I feeling chilly. She disappointed but forbearing. Also loaning me 200 francs.

In Paris "one" allowed to be fussy. The ego gloating a little.


18. Waking today wondering why B. In montage method he using for huge Paris history. Juxtaposing *Les noms des rues*, Paris street names section. On *Prostitution* chapter. It making perfect sense to abut *Mode* and *Passages*, arcades. Association also obvious between *Daumier*—political cartoonist—and *Mouvement social*. On second look. It not *Les noms des rues de Paris*, Paris street names. But simply *Les rues de Paris*, Paris streets. Juxtaposed on *Prostitution* chapter. Association banal to point of prurient. Given it implying. Any (female) walker. Possibly on way to sexual market. Which banality seemingly contesting. Alleged objectivity of history-montage method. Wherein author saying nothing. Only endlessly oneirically conjuncting. Facts and anecdotes. For purpose of shocking unconscious knowing. Into realm of conscious recognition.

But can unconscious. Be trusted.

All this to avoid discussing what. *Still* can't bring myself to say. On morning after young compatriot P. Taking me to Deux-Magots. Old hangout. Of Sartre & Co. Hot summer evening. Leaves tinkling. Sky: powder. Sitting inside. Nearly empty. Outer terrasse full of wealthy tourists. Red plush and mirrors. Mosaic floor. Scalloped pattern of beige interlocking fans. Repeated on pinkish marble mirror frames. One woman in black décolletée leotard. Very large breasts. P ordering a litre. Though penniless.

Insisting on paying. While I admiring brushcut. Dusky high cheek-bones. Slenderness.

Then suddenly I blurting out. How yesterday taking body. Hysterical with sleeplessness. To lunch with administrators of leisure lottery studio. New tight French shoes purchased at pricey Bon Marché. Paris's first department store. Where faubourg ladies. Already fighting. Barely post-Commune. Over ventes des blancs, linen sales. Plus Beatles's-style jacket. Slightly faded wide-legged black cotton pants. Male administrator tall and fuzzy. Female magnificently expensive Paris hippy. Décolletée Indian shirt. Jet curls. Overcooked fish. Disintegrating into bits. Between fork and heavy fishknife. Difficulty of eating adding to need. For justifying anglo accent. Therefore I vigorously claiming support of québécois Independence. Magnificent woman exuding perfume. Smiling encouragement. Gently leading me to revealing complex nature. Of family tree. Only little French. Also English. Irish. Huron. Fairly typical mix. I grinning. *Sûrement* murmuring male leisure lottery director. Staring nonplussed.

P's cropped head back in hilarity.

They got their money's worth. Adding to console: the French don't understand people can have lost touch. With their history.


19. Bastille Day. Dusk. Looking out at rainwashed streets. A policeman. Then soldier in khakis. With peaked pillbox of French military. Pacing down block. All traffic headed towards Les Invalides. For fireworks. The soldier looking up at window. Continuing down street. Looking up again. Quickly shutting outer blind or store. Feeling paranoid. Feeling desolate for feeling that.

S's sick of me.

All day the army on display. Endless columns. Rows and rows abreast. Live or on TV. Moving along Champs-Élysées in tanks. On foot. On horses. Perfect shiny uniforms. Varying with function. Casques bleus for Bosnia. Colonial tans for Africa. Army fatigues for regular. Jets flying in formation. Very low. Trailing tri-coloured exhaust. Over platform near Arc de Triomphe. Ill-looking socialist president. Robust right-wing prime minister. Spectacle conjuring up word republic. As opposed to chez nous. We being subjects with foreign queen on dollars. Is there a republican way of occupying space. People speaking as if believing in sound of their voice. A Frenchman when speaking. Waxing rhetorical. Giving full seriousness to what's issuing. Almost caressingly. From mouth. Americans in restaurants. Shouting confidentially.

Now on TV military parading over. Interviews with homeless people in Gare du Nord. Each citoyen(ne) standing up and proclaiming her opinion. Male hooker in rapid articulate manner. Analytic. Yet introducing wistful note. Wishing to have an ami, lover. Un petit appartement pour ne plus venir ici, a small apartment so not having to come here. Naturellement a bourgeois(e) having last word. In good leather shoes with little wedge heels. Telling homeless kids their parents rotten. Comment peut-on mettre un gamin á la porte, how can you throw out a kid. The "kids" laughing at her mockingly. But you can see the hurt in their eyes.

20. P interrupting me. Via fax. Having committed terrible "sins." I thinking: AIDS. Though French statistically safer. This turning out to be ridiculous. Night nice and mellow. On TV. Man has pants down. String attached to zi-zi. Coming out of boxer shorts. Someone pulling it this way and that. Talk-show audience laughing.

Later meeting her at LE DRUGSTORE SAINT-GERMAIN. Her little brown multi-ringed ear. Leaning over counter. Asking pale bespectacled woman pharmacist. About some kind of testing. For anemia. Then growing angry. At my loudly questioning price. Just like an American! We walking down several quays. Crossing place de la Bastille. Immense traffic circle. Up narrow street. Her room yellow. Studio of dreams. On tranquil little courtyard. Rue de la Roquette. Named after two prisons. In turn named after lettuce. Once abundantly growing there. Sheets with yellow rosebuds. Hung high on rack over stove. P nodding below. At woman from Portugal. Who in purchasing little room. Erroneously understanding. Access to toilet. P sharing hers. Shared as well with old couple.

Coughing through wall. TB she saying. Mock-dramatic. I'm afraid I'll get it. Should I call the authorities.

After which she walking me back. To left bank. Then walking back to right bank again. Another fifty minutes. Albeit past midnight. Walking all over Paris. Any time of night. I kissing her dusky cheek. Softly downed in streetlight. Tenderly. Then going to shake her hand. This garnering a slap. Retreating to cushion. Opening Balzac's *Girl with Golden Eyes*. Duvet also on her neck. My reflection. In row of convex mirrors. More age of the marquise.

Still looking pretty good.

21. A nasty catarrh. Displaying—I mean explaining—lack of dynamism. Hardly dragging out of bed. Feeling like weeks since I sleeping. Because day fairly nice grey and breezy. Going out anyway. But only to noisy Sèvres-Babylone café. Devouring passersby with eyes. Gold ankle chain passing treetrunk with fish-beating heart. Gypsy's long flowered skirt. Something red on nicely shaped arm. Extended begging. At métro. Man again selling *Macadam*, *Pavement*.

I opening *Le Monde*. Young Algerian professor expelled. Just as doctoral defence coming up. But not French wife and kids. Slender woman in white pantsuit. Immaculate straight-cut hair. Crossing street in direction of art-deco hotel opposite. Façade draped in grapes. Songbirds singing in them. Only mouth giving away woman's age. Tight. Slightly turned-down at corners. Mouth of disappointment.

Curve of disappointment on own mouth. Spied recently in café mirror. Making me want to shape up immediately. At the time watching the québécoise C's lovely full lips. Even when distressed. Producing moue of self-mocking humour. Mocking French mocking québécois way of speaking. Nasalizing pain, bread. Mouth half-opened. Instead of lips rounding over aspirated consonant. Like a kiss. Parisians surely owing beauty. To ubiquity of mirror. Barely post-Revolution—most homes having two. While in England—rare. Even in châteaux.

22. But energy *back!* With brio drinking strong coffee. Eating soft bread and jam. Butter spread so thick. Leaving teethmarks in it. Wishing breakfast would never end. Returning to divan. B falling open at chapter on flâneur. Lost in 19th-century crowd. Yet capable of haunting. Being man (sic) in full possession of individuality. Contrary to onlooker. Who under influence of crowd. No longer One.

Showering I feeling in middle. Neither One. Nor entirely bleeding into context either. I.e. haunting only concierge. In turn haunting me. With strong personality. Soon to be ringing bell. Convinced "one" sleeping til noon. When it agreed she bringing mail. This somehow causing resentment. Yesterday—having failed to close the store, blind again. After peeking out early. She knocking belligerently. Prematurely. On door. Dragging lemony antiseptic smell behind. To make matters worse. I wearing old pyjama top.

Crime here: upsetting a routine. As in colleagues from chez nous. Last night surprising twice. First—by showing up (without wanting to stay over). Second—liking projected little bk on murdered women! She in white blouse and long skirt. Very contained. Basic female requirement. For balanced heterosexual couple. He with brilliant high forehead. Lapsing into English. Walking down du Bac. Complaining about ubiquity of visual image. E.g. Gulf War in real time. On TV. Giving faux-sense of democracy. Because *in reality* "one" passively absorbing. Compared to. Say. Here he looking round meaningfully. Compared to certain less anecdotal more analytic narratives. Requiring participatory i.e. *truly* democratic effort. Maybe. I thinking. Straightening in boutique façade mirror. Then passing cops by café—I whispering speak French so they not asking for visa. Forgetting québécois accents.

Arm 'n arm we strolling. Chatting. Chatting. Passing hotel façade on which vines also gossiping. Climbing familiarly on shoulders of plumtrees. Down Cherche-Midi, Noon-Seeking Street. Old Roman road. Where sun rarely shining. Rarely hitting aging black dresses. Of tired boutique women. Into Roman restaurant. Divine antipasto. Fresh mozzarella. Tomatoes with basil. Spinach. Mush-rooms. Limas in vinaigrette. Garlicky aubergines. Veal in sauce. Tiramisu. Sipping grappa. Waiter hearing accents. Gesturing to-ward terrasse. Your compatriot's out there. Meaning famous québécoise pop singer Diane Dufresne. Chez nous we calling her la Diva. Though once accidentally falling off stage. At Paris Olympia.

Très cher I telling P later. She saying stop fetishizing price tags. Value here measured otherwise. She's right! Cold gone com-pletely.

23. Waking again at 5:30a. Guessing time by density of traffic. More than by light. Laddering spaces between upper slats of store. Cars racing. Then—as long as 30 seconds—silence. Later constant buzz and roar of city passing into blood. Until well past midnight. When at last nearly quiet.

If here only a week or two—repressing it all completely. In-stead of trying to absorb. Producing that frown in bistro mirrors. Not having entirely mastered. French pleasure-balancing trick. E.g. countering hangover. Like woman leisure lottery director. With simple filet mignon. Light sauce. One glass of right wine. Taken in deep insistent breath. No distractions. No deep-fried onion rings. Thousand Island dressing. Similar specialized well-being. Served at l'onglerie, for nails. La parfumerie, for perfume. Le bottier, for boots. La ganterie, for gloves. Even men wearing perfume. Purses. Little tootsies cosseted in nice silk socks.

Last evening I possibly also beautiful for minute. In wide-bottomed pants. Semi-bobbed hair. Strolling to Pont-Neuf. Stand-ing straighter to avoid scraggly North American look. Reflecting on why outer advantage. Improving inner sense of self. In turn likely serving clarity of thinking. Leaning over bridge. Taking in sunset. Through partly cloudy sky. On glass-and-iron roof. Of magnificent Grand Palais. Built for 1900 World Exhibition. At curve of river. Then strolling back again. Walking up Rennes. Sudden cold rain. Abruptly showering half-naked torso. Of young man sitting. Bent forward. On cement promontory. Near Prix

Unique. Displaying back scored with large deep scars. Likely burns. I hurrying down curved white Grenelle. Stopping only to look in display window of expensive men's shop. Across from studio.

*Something strange going on there!* Mannequins in unbelievably well-made suits. Handstitched lapels. Switching constantly. From window to window. Now one mannequin arm in knife-sharp cuff. Gesturing magnanimously to other. In neighbouring display window. As if some kind of code. Or narrative. Generated by understanding. Men having between them.

24. And happy as lark. Sitting in dream café! On modest little market square. Near cimitière Montparnasse. Place Edgar-Quinet. After romantic French poet. Whose Paris. B saying. Haunted by lyric dancing towers. Cathedrals kneeling before sepulchres. Monuments combing columns of golden hair. On shoulders.

But only ordinary working people crossing square. Market stalls. News stands. Métro. Wooden table near window. Men and women reading left-leaning *Libération*. Outside on terrasse loving couple. He stroking stroking her hair. Very gently. Two rosy-cheeked schoolgirls.

I opening more intellectual *Le Monde*. Article tracing European indifference toward current horror in Bosnia. Back to centuries-old Christian hate of Muslims. Beginning with crusade-guru Urban II. Convincing flocks to leave what they loving. Châteaux. Land. (Wives.) Taking up sword. To search for Grail. Quest marking beginning of Hell. For Arab peoples.

Brisk wind blowing. It could rain a little. Trees looking like stunted aspens. Turning up leaves. Café filling with people coming in from work. Older socialists on right. He drinking beer. She hot milk. Very sweet-looking. Talking about whatever old socialists talking about. She from time to time venturing opinion. He shooting down immediately. Guy on terrasse stroking lover's shiny hair.

Watching—it occurring to me. Movement over square. Less real-time mirror. Than cinema of gestures. Pointing beyond frame. E.g. empty chair opposite. Possibly implying how "one" aching for her. Simultaneously expanding grammatically. To take in time's "progress." At margins of perception: guy on terrasse. Now kissing girl. Passionately. Tiny vans. Parking on narrow sidewalks. Economy of bustle. Keeping Paris going. Axed on verb. The French-language way. Which way Gertrude Stein miming. Walking poodle Basket up windy Raspail. Trumpeting that by emphasizing predicates. She inventing the 20th.

Now man on ladder washing awning. Inscribed *Couture*. Swilling away soot falling on everything. Insidious film. Eternally shadowing grey to black. Postwar Paris nearly black city. Sand-blasted back again. Time as soot. The only place to paint de Chirico saying. *Such shades of grey.*

As if to illustrate own time-discombobulation. Walking home from new café. Later. I noticing bright neoned fronts of LE DÔME and LE SELECT. Where Hemingway declaring. Paris belonging to him. Situated only few blocks from leisure lottery studio. Reinforcing sense of having stumbled into some mythological space. Trying to negotiate way along narrow passage between cars. Parked on sidewalk. Impossible to break into nice free stroll. Legs suddenly trembling. Violently. Another relapse. Or just overdose of caffeine.

Raining in Sarajevo.

25. S and friend the publisher popping into new café. Suddenly I feeling in *Paris I expecting*. Espresso machine bubbling. Delicious nape of redhead across room. Eating pommes parisiennes, parsley fried potatoes. And cutlet. S talking of meaning of hope. Given contingency of mondialisation. Reducing life to economics. Publisher deploring epoch's cynicism. Citing fashion industry. Models in loosely woven silk "sacking" fringed at bottom. Held shut with silver safety pins. Miming dress of homeless. Albeit every fashion parade still ending with bride. Redhead getting up and leaving. Subject changing to ambiguous article in *Libé*. On gay rights. Editor implying à la limite doing IT. May be illegal.

S leaving with him. Crossing little square. Being hosed down after market. Stepping out of frame. Into Montparnasse cemetery.

I in a dream state. Ordering more espresso. Before getting up and strolling. Toward asymmetrical steeples. Of lovely Saint-Sulpice. Pausing. Watching "verbs." Pigeons. Nuns. Water blowing from Four Bishops' Fountain. Like incense. Thinking of Stein's predilection for predicates. Which predicates—in multiplying—soaking up surroundings. Until mysteriously inflating subject (narrator). Into huge transparent shadow.

Day still mild. Slightly grey.

Yet another coffee. Then strolling over pont Marie. Clouds above rushing into dusk. Bateaux-Mouches casting floodlights on façades of buildings along river. Like graffiti. Words *Écriture blanche*, white or neutral writing. Conjuring French Stein-opposite; writing so "objective" or factual—narrator seeming ghost. Or refraction. Strong warm wind. Whipping dandruff onto black shirt. Elevator to C's tiny studio. Opening on rooftop terrasse. Under pink Paris sky. We from chez nous. Gazing down dreamily. On reflections. From passing bateaux-mouches. While drinking Chablis. Chablis. Ch-a-a-a-blis. Eating artichokes. Lot, monkfish with beurre. Raspberries. Crème fraîche. Then C's hand on shoulder. Heading rapidly. Toward realm of anecdote.

Instead. Creeping out wine-sodden. Grabbing last métro. Thinking B saying anecdotes. Only facts re-remembered. Dressed up. In contingency of raconteur's establishment. Outside train window. Métro officials ridding benches of clochards. Trying to catch forty winks. While still having place to sit. Off at du Bac. And sleeping sleep of "one." Who's taken her pleasure well. Notwithstanding small patch of eczema.

26. Waking. Wondering if metabolism changing due to new environment. Huge appetite for breakfast. Having suddenly disappeared. A couple of tartines. No thought of lunch. Or eating rest of what usually eating for breakfast. Yoghurt. Ditto way of moving. Trimmer. Red mop smooth. Strolling to Palais-Royal. Former home of Colette. Old hedonist. Knowing how to take pleasures of the body. Without ruining her skin. Pale-with-something-darker-under. She

grooming fifty minutes daily. Standing by mirror. Automatically straightening sagging hip. Raising drooping neck. Before sitting at desk. And writing fifty books.

I entering from behind. Through crumbly passage end. Very 18th-century. Noticing my derrière sticking out. In large mirrored door with little cherubs dancing on corners. Across rue de Beaujolais. Mechanical toys in window. Snow falling on gazebo. Couple waltzing in it. Emerging into lovely treed garden. Lindens. Planes. Entirely symmetrical with colonnade of three-sided arcade. Fountains gurgling lazily. Birds singing everywhere. Old Colette's magnificent aubergine head. Above. Sniffing. Touching. Listening. To very end. Despite pain of arthritis. Heavy immovable body. Irritating boys. Shitting below.

Anyway. Standing under arcade bordering square. Staring at pastries. Looking like flat dented cooks' hats. Chocolate poured over. When young French man suddenly popping up. Very neat in blue sweater. Fair features aglow with hunger. I'm not kidding. Sans blague. He saying apologetically. I'm starving. Also possibly eczema. I looking around grumpily. Afraid he grabbing changepurse. If taking it out. Noting he neater than me. Also thinking he sincere.

Strolling back through Tuileries. Through sun-mottled leaves. The light exacerbating effect of mottled bark on trees. Like army fatigues. Slightly worn heels. Crossing pont Royal. Up rue du Bac. Noting in expensive men's clothing stores across from studio. Suited mannequin now standing in window on right. Headlessness half-hidden behind newspaper.

27. Evening in studio. Sinking deeper on cushion. Below usual stiff little dogs. Usual street-cleaner with green vacuum hose. Swilling refuse into sewer. Part of underground maze of streets. Cellars. Grottos. Of whole underground city. Sunset behind buildings providing backdrop. To surface. So storefront across street becoming clearer. As dusk advancing. Store lights coming on. Mannequin in window. Now *stuffed suit*. Sitting on sofa. Lit-up globe for head. While on lit-up screen in studio. War. Eternally returning. That great scar:

Documentarist implying certain prosecutors. Having condemned people to camps. Still sitting on court benches. Then clip of French village. Suddenly re-remembering. Busload of disappearing children.

Second documentary—from chez nous! *La Vie des Esquimaux* (sic). Child in igloo. Learning how to sew. Looking up wondrously at mother. Also sitting sewing in cotton housedress. The whole somehow like white suburban family scene. Standard in '50s *Chatelaine* magazine. I.e. *FRAMED*. By contingency of director's establishment. Having apparently disremembered. Residential schooling. For Aboriginals.

We all having something to cover up.

28. Is it optical illusion. Male mannequin in window across street this morning. Now on feet. Still faceless. Behind him dark-wood bench. Where previously sitting. Hand "resting" on it. As soon as it stops raining—employee stepping out. Washing display windows. Behind yellow bench of bus stop. On which woman. Large black bag over shoulder. Black dress. Pearls. Beside her on bus shelter wall. Ad for French winter coats. Featuring "Indian" in headdress. Also waste can. With suspicious package sticking out. Titillating. What if all the birds were to suddenly stop singing. Within walled gardens of the magnificent hôtels particuliers, private mansions along rue de Varenne. In warning. OF IMMINENT EXPLOSION. Sometimes—behind walls blind onto sidewalk—a village street almost. Lined with residences for family and servants. Now two more faubourg specimens standing by "Indian." Identical mother/daughter. Each very slender. Each wearing pearls. Elegant calf-length pale summer dresses. Chatting complicitly.

I love this quarter wrote one English writer. Indeed replied another. You are among the fossilized remnants of the old régime.

29. Sky bright blue. Exiting into street. Thinking marvellous surely to be had. Looking up at balcony of post-Second Empire building. On corner. Blonde not reappearing. Descending into métro. To visit one of those old passages. B speaking of. Out at porte Saint-Denis.

Crumbling neighbourhood. In shadow of triumphal arch raised by Louis XIV. Breton finding beautiful. Arch façades sculpted with happy female faces. Conjuring victories. Or weeping. Under which C waiting. Several "business transactions" also taking place. Including two men in black. Shaking hands with white packets in them. Looking round. Fake surreptitious.

We heading down Saint-Denis. Mid merchants. Pushing trolleys full of cheap clothes. Women in doorways. Not necessarily young. Dress or colour-detail announcing lush: stacked sweater or huge breasts in little lace corset. Or classy: geometric haircuts. Ripe: lace stockings held in place with garters. Just below short skirts. In window—artist model mannequins. Ultra-flexible joints. Wearing only boots and frizzy hair. Guy with dice game on sidewalk. Trying to draw us in. Then screaming paranoically not to take his picture. Crowds of walkers. A few conjuring up contemporaneous flâneur. I.e. *stoned.*

Right on slanted square. Groups of men huddled. Joking. Bartering excitedly. Mostly from "the south." Three Hathors with big ears and little friezes on square Egyptian hats. Over passage entrance. Built to celebrate Bonaparte's entering Egypt. I saying certain old passages having walls and ceilings covered in marble. Gold leaf. Paintings. Mirrors. Saying windows once stained and hung in magnificent brocades. Saying how artful once the furniture. How fragrant the flowers. Musical the birds. A kind of public salon. Her lovely lips smiling. Albeit possibly nonplussed this anglaise. Cognizant of Paris she not knowing.

More and more I loving it.

Unfortunately—through passage door. Battered—not to say smashed up—marble floors. Glass roofs filthy. Rows of heating pipes. Ugly shades of brindle. No sign of Egyptian-style pilasters once decorating storefronts. Selling cheap textiles. Uniforms. Pastel polyester underwear. One rather marvellous garden shop. Every yard bench/statuary/cupid/pot. Covered in dark green moss. As if ghosts of themselves. Exiting back on Saint-Denis. More throngs. More trolleys full of clothing. Before us again. Porte Saint-Denis.

Where—back when king entering city. Three live naked young women posing as sirens. Under curved part of arch. No longer gate. Instead sticking up in middle. Of ever-expanding city. Therefore completely useless. As Breton pointing out. Uselessness adding. To convulsive beauty. For Cardinal of surrealism.

Saint Denis also walking this way. Carrying his head. I informing C.

She lighting cigarette. Mobile lips. Ironic.

30. Looking out. Noticing for first time. Discreetness of shop signs along street. E.g. exclusive men's clothing shop insignia. So tiny. Unreadable from studio. *Artisan Parfumeur* also writ smallish on awning. Most criard, loud: sign right below window. Little flag or banner at right angle to wall. Aggressively projecting. Profile of young man in black peaked cap. Over very androgynous under- and lounging-clothes. In boutique window. Run by growth-challenged guy with brilliantined hair. Complaining about vibrations. When workman drilling in studio. *Un pédé*—concierge now saying. Of former. Her dark mouth. Curling in disgust.

Going through lobby. I believing she hates me. Giving dirty looks. Laughing uproariously when I asking where to put *vidange*. As we saying chez nous. For garbage. Here vidange meaning slop-pail. Should have said *poubelle*. Also having once more failed to hear her ring. Bringing up mail. Due to playing music from Maghrebia. Or arias on rightist Catholic station. Or trailer-truck roaring by. She screaming I never in. I trying to expand shoulders. In manner of republican. Though heart beating rapidly. Predecessor saying she screaming at him. Too. Coming down staircase. Carrying *his* poubelle. In bag of over-large format.

Hot. Strolling down Raspail. Boutique windows. Repeating pregnant outfits. Pearl-encrusted wedding bodices. Copper pots. Rugs. Divans. Left on Gertrude Stein's street. Stumbling on *second* nice café. In week! By small triangular square. Group of youngish winos. Bottles of cheap rosé stashed in greenish bronze fountain. From end of Second Empire. Or later Belle Époque. When hygiene suddenly an issue. Some fountains B saying. Even dispensing hot water. On putting coin in slot. Caryatids round empty basin's edge. Bent back heads holding up top or little roof. Circular wrought form repeated in old pissoirs. Kiosques. All over Paris. Now mostly empty moulds.

Taking table near window. Musing how to deal with concierge. Maybe buying flowers. Feeling so lethargic. Café filling up. Young French lesbian. White shirt. Jeans unravelled at bottom. Wonderful mouth. Asking quietly for time. Argentinean woman. With man looking like Belmondo. Carefully forming French words. Over teeth. Like mine. Unfortunately ambience destroyed. By group of anglos. From chez nous. Entering with Scandinavian girlfriends. One redfaced guy. Crumpled linen suit. Loudly. Obstreperously. Speaking of his Art. Simultaneously somehow maintaining fake bashful look. By means of throwing back head and closing eyes. While mouth opening wide. Enumerating successes.

But. Loving this state of absolute unfeeling. Putting "one" in total posture of receptivity.

Why shouldn't the flâneur be stoned.


31. Diary drifting along on brow of lethargy. Paris sunny. Deserted. En vacances. Iron curtains pulled down in front of shops. L'ARTISAN PARFUMEUR across street with white clapboard curtain. Someone having scrawled *Waste* on it in English. Conjuring associate chez nous. Claiming to be allergic. Loudly complaining if someone scented. Sitting next to her on bus. What would she do here.*

A long dog peeing lengthily against one of those green wrought-brass structures. Between two maples on boulevard strip. Probably old wastecan. Curved top like sentry box. Usual Modern Style floral patterns in relief. Emptiness of background. Ennui. Turning on TV. In Sarajevo people strolling in fog. Suddenly bayonetted and thrown in river. Then concierge loudly ringing bell. Handing in letter.

*Oh no. *She* coming. Tomorrow!

34

32. Houseguest initially quite helpful.

I falling asleep on cushion. Feeling warm and happy. Buzz of things happening. In all-white kitchen. Electronic coffee-maker. Dishwasher. Something nice in oven. Things getting organized. Programming fax and e-mail. For transatlantic missives. De rigueur for contemporary artist. Then arguing re: cost of Vittel. When *I*— only wanting to escape. Down unfamiliar streets. Hugging walls of courtyards. Hiding Paris's unconscious. That tiny knight with round knuckle-shield. Behind Cherche-Midi gate. Or Pinocchio leaning forward. Nose touching floor. In Hôtel Lutétia alcove.

Unfortunately she following. Down stairs. Past concierge. Sitting with radio to ear. Who laughing outright. At overall. Covering houseguest's ample form. Not to mention round-bowl haircut. In hot street—I concentrating on rooftops. Chimney pots. Little greenhouses. Terrasses. Treetips. Lean-tos. Receptor saucers. Grilles. Co-existing in laissez-faire manner. That Paris traditionally ignored by building codes. Practically surrealist. I explaining to houseguest. Who trying to be convivial. Pointing from café chair on sidewalk. To "anarchic" little cave-like opening. Moulded high on chic Lutétia façade opposite. Oh that only art-deco detail. I commenting acidly. Adding *surely* anarchy more spontaneous. Than some architect's goal-oriented dream.

Just then faubourg woman passing. Holding daschund tight to body. Shoulders uncharacteristically hunched. Head intensely forward. Dog's head protruding from middle of woman's body. Held jutting forward. Just like hers. Equally intense. Expression of much-loved child. Or gargoyle.

We bursting out laughing.


33. Blessed floating state now also fucked up. By scalp. Hands. Feet so itchy. Could tear skin off. Lifting camisole. Seeing several bites and pinholes. As if some bug having been interrupted. In act of sucking blood. There following panic of the traveller: frantic changing of bedding. Washing of sheets. Hair. Body. More likely an allergy. With haphazard flea. Into conjecture.

Then sitting on canapé. Smiling ironically.

C ringing bell. Stopping in foyer to pass time of day with concierge. I had her purring. She declaring. Coming through door. Il faut les jazzer, you have to chat them up. Bill in envelope also de rigueur. I nodding knowingly. Wondering how much. Frying little pink rabbit bits. Purchased at farmers' market. On median strip of boulevard. Beyond Banque de France. Stepping in like entering. Another economy completely. Rhythm of bargaining. People leaning forward. Ritually repeating: bonjour Messieurs Dames. Shrewd. Excitement. About what's alive. O la belle salade. Vous me faites un prix, make me a deal. Oakleafed. Curly. Mâche. People milling. Laughing. Argumentative. Over turbot. Little darling shrimps. Blond Norman. Swallowing herring whole. Ten kinds of mushrooms. Fifteen of olives. Redfaced kerchiefed peasant. Fingers gnarled as display of deeply fragrant roots. Quiche. Thick and light. Bubbling cheese on top. Butcher twitching nose bunny-like. Cutting off little rabbit's moustaches. Mon fils, my son saying his mother. But on TV cooks saying. Markets not as before. Supermarkets killing them. Once great Les Halles. Reduced to wax figures representing peasants. Pushing barrows of produce. In alcove of église Saint-Eustache.

Still rabbit delicious. Marinating in thyme. In closed plastic dish. Whole afternoon. It being difficult to fail. Given quality of products. Washed down by Brouilly. Contributed by C. Digestif on canapé. She and I pointedly bemoaning. Quantities of tourists. For benefit of houseguest. One hundred thousand daily. Television saying. Germans. Brightly dressed Scandinavians. Holding hands in clean homogenous pairs. Good for economy. But Parisians tiring. Of being asked directions. Then item about franc. Which French identifying with. As if it themselves—C piping up. Currently in crisis. To profit of—Germany. Again. Widespread concern re: projected unified monetary system in Europe. I.e. re: feared resurgence of German power. But for we from chez nous. Falling franc a bonanza. Rendering our pathetic currency feasible.

Twas the weak franc between wars. Permitting expatriates to flock here for nourishment. Good food. Wine. Slow time. Soaking up ambience of still-19th backdrop. To invent the 20th. Then dollar crashing. People running from café to café. Shouting I'm getting outta here. While I can.

Guest putting on earphones.


34. On canapé. Missing empty space. Space of observation. Of time. Slipping into nothingness. Therefore bottling up what B calling tedium vitae. Supposedly reflecting increasingly alienating division of labour. In 19th. Now leading to useless pathos. Like: "I not coping very well with life." State of floating requiring letting *down* boundaries. Absorbing context completely. Which "one" can do inasmuch as alone. No ties. No domestic worries (action). No familiar context. Sending back authoritative unsatisfactory images.

She's got her earphones on. Again. Strolling to Musée Rodin. In one of those lovely faubourg walled gardens. Birds singing. Blooming arbori. Calais burghers. Plotting. Balzac. Dreaming up *Girl with Golden Eyes*. Behind azaleas. Grey sky. Sun. No—Napoléon's golden dome. In distance. Houseguest behind. In and out of every square and oval salon. Full of objects. Posturing as subjects: muscular hands of God. Men at arms. Heroic frank-eyed women. I stumbling on little grouping of Rodin's girlfriend Camille Claudel's wrenching figures. Luminous green marble women. Leaning towards each other. Conversationally. Obsessively. Plus small bronze female figures. Muscles tensed. Holding hands and jumping. Into large marble wave. More ephemeral. Than R's confident chunks. I thinking. Staring. One's thoughts thinking this. Seeming special. Unique. As they should do in museum. When houseguest stepping up. Declaring same sentiments exactly. Which scenario repeated. Before Rodin's sculpture of couple entwined. Male penis passing right through woman lover. Unless that thing sticking out her back. Little satyr's tail. Anyway—I standing there. Enjoying sexual bi-ambivalence. When houseguest's flashbulb going off. Taking me from behind.

Later—walking to Camille's workshop. Île-Saint-Louis. Wind blowing through leaves. Footpaths. Quiet old studios. Overlooking water. Most peaceful place in Paris. Where *termina sa brève carrière d'artiste, et commença la longue nuit d'internement,* her brief career as artist ending in long night of internment. I thinking of way to tell houseguest. She making me feel framed. Then she taking me. Again. Reading plaque. And again. By café with decades-old signs: CAFÉ 10c LA TASSE (now 10F is cheap). AVEC PETIT VERRE 15c & 20c. On sloping cobblestone terrasse. Just feet away from workshop. Maybe Camille coming here to breakfast.

Unless anorexic.

At next café table. Three Parisians speaking of opera. Smooth accents slipping over s's. Blonde older Sybil. Cardigan over shoulders. Two men. One likely gay. Raving about new American diva. Precision of *her* accent. Expression on her face. Juste avant de mourir, just before dying. Librettically speaking. Reminding me of young French woman cellist. Seen in new-music festival chez nous. Whose mocking arias ever more hysterical. Until cello bow. In fake unfortunate gesture. Getting hung on her nose.

Some frames more interesting than others.


35. Lethargy. Place Edgar-Quinet. Nearly floating. Again. Over divine espresso. Over divine Montparnasse. *She leaving tomorrow!* So at last recovering empty space. Though first must needs to market. De rigueur for artist. Since at least Baudelaire. Having decided to submit projected little Bk of Murdered Women. To S's friend the editor. He now going by in sunglasses. Two days' growth of beard. Avoiding looking at me. Everything here's like that. No contact.

Image likewise de rigueur. Therefore crossing over. To hairdresser on edge of square. Where once seeing delicious nape of redhead entering. Now only clients with frosty pageboys. Discussing baptismal gowns for grandchildren. Leafing through catalogue. Models all transsexual! He also very stagey. We arguing about price. Not the one posted on window. Listen he saying. This my price when working in 7th. I.e. in pricey faubourg. Je n'ai pas baissé, I am not any worse. For moving to 'Parnasse. Nor will he do as I wishing. Hair needs movement. He declaring—scissor points wide open. To calm him I offering conversation. Complaining chevelure terne, hair dull and tired. Since coming to Paris. It's the tour Eiffel he quipping. *Very tiring*. Meaning 1,652 steps up. Or meaning. He bored.

In three-sided mirror. Haircut effectively moving. In line from nape to cheekbone. Smooth. Yet enough play to encourage natural waves. A little height in front. Neck very clean. Like cuts of women on old Modern Style posters. Walking down windswept rue du Départ. By Montparnasse station. Cheap hotels and bars for people disembarking. With nowhere to go. Reflection in windows déjà-vu ca 1970. Face hawking time. Soft. Vulnerable breast in cotton push-up bra. Under jersey moulée. The young Deneuve. Likewise back in fashion.

36. She's gone!

And the sun is shining through the slats of the store. Walking across studio. Cranking ivory handle. Is that guy watching. Sitting in cheap shoes on bench across the street. Crank it down again. Robberies rife in August. Ils en profitent, take advantage. Of people on vacation. Concierge saying. Standing erect on pale diagonally cut marble tiles of lobby. Before opening heavy door. And shouting MERDE with dark mouth. At poor woman. Possibly from l'est, Eastern Europe. Trying to creep in. To sell her wares of lace. Never hearing MERDE that loud before.

Then she inviting me. Into little mahogany cage. Table laden with flowers from inhabitants of upper studios and suites. Plus glass cabinet with hardcover collection of Verlaine. Picture of child on top. Absent the husband. Leisure lottery people mentioning. Only old grey Persian in armchair. Looking straight ahead.

Hearing nothing. Total lack of windows. So no traffic. Though traffic not bothering. Like it used to. Albeit very early this morning. Car alarm going off at intervals. Followed by usual hyperbole of commerce. Small white vans. Firetrucks. Ambulances. Concierge pointing to picture. Saying child dying due to hospital maltreatment. Therefore she leaving very early Thursdays. To visit boy's tomb. Many buses out. On outskirts.

I climbing back upstairs. Guilty. Of not resisting. Putting her in here. She being unique Parisian type. Perfected at height of Revolution. When working people suddenly speaking out. Thin junkie guy. Still on bench below. Capable of climbing on bus stop and into studio window. Once I disappearing. Down rue du Bac. Not yet floating. Again. But feeling okay. Autumn in air. Intuition always to be in Paris then. To buy a suit of black. To dream. To write. To wander. Being subject with foreign queen on dollars. I.e. nostalgic. For distance. Of 19th-century novel. As in *I* purveying P's bare arm. Holding up phone. Simultaneously trying to grasp some point in future. By eclipsing *I* of certain early-20th travelling republicans. Who having abolished comma. Drawing all of us. In portrait of about three words. But if comma of translation disappearing. What of French-speaking America remaining.

37. Already yellow light of melancholy autumn. Yesterday leaning over pont Marie. The Seine a golden tint. Heartbreaking in its beauty. Writing this in journal. Tracing square around it. Later reading in *Le Monde*. Two Africans strolling there. Stopped and asked for papers. One panicking. Jumping into river. And drowning. Albeit papers in order. Having only photocopy on him.

And I seeing nothing. Though pausing at length. Gazing at white surface of river. Blinking back ironically. Then—given ubiquity of cops—taking circuitous route back. Via les Invalides. Past Rodin's studio. Where poet Rilke briefly living. Feeling under lozenge of orange air. Small dark lick of cold. Also—despite extreme beauty of day—nothing marvellous to report. Except large cooked

artichoke. Resplendent with purple green clipped wings. For pre-
ceding fresh pasta. Turned in spoon of tomato sauce. Rilke's words
in head. *This is what I want: to float on the waves / Unattached to
time.*

38. It occurring to me—state of feeling-less. Precursive to state
of floating. Possibly problematic. Because in hovering/observ-
ing. "One" passively absorbing little external details. Arbitrarily
pre-selected. By Paris "one" expecting. Terrasse still vacation-
deserted. Pink beaded goblet. Next tallish empty glass. Word
ORANGINE sweating on it. Plus water carafe with sliced oranges.
Advertising another product. Simple outlines on plain or empty
backgrounds. Like those early-century Modern Style posters of
pretty women. On white backing. Still found wrapped in cello-
phane on Paris quays. Which white or empty sets. B saying. Be-
speaking bourgeois desire. Not to hear rumblings of coming war.
Himself committing suicide. While fleeing Nazis. Over Spanish
border.

   I ordering more Kir. Sky paling behind LA GAÎTÉ. Where old
Colette formerly performing. Her early turn-of-20th work Modern Style too. Les *Claudines* emphasizing silhouettes. Projecting
in simplicity of appearance. Some new kind of writing. Walking
up Raspail in pinkness of dusk. I musing whether all ends of
centuries requiring—résumé of surfaces. Back in studio. Looking out at façade opposite. With lucious blonde in there somewhere. Its indeterminate pasted-on decor. Rejection of periods.
As if time adrift. A bastard. Thinking: at least now no war in
Europe.

   Then on television: Bosnia.

39. Morning. Still dark because shutters down. Me lying here thinking how to write. More progressive chronicle. Maybe author déjà
vu by narrator. Instead of usual reverse. Permitting latter to float
beyond limitations. Biases. Of former. Grey frowning sky. Then
bright sun replacing grey between store's varnished slats. It going

to be one of those clear scintillating almost-autumn days. Can't wait to "live" it.

Getting up and putting store to awning position. Y-awning. Letting in a little light. Yet keeping place cool. Over tops of buildings. Clouds whipping up. Thinking I telling a lot of lies in this diary.

Pretending wanting love (when wanting to be alone). To be working. When sitting on cushion. Then noticing also inadvertently lying about discreetness of signs. Along street. Perfume shop store not having one *discreet* sign. Barely visible. As thinking earlier. But TWO signs in gold. Made to somehow appear discreet. On shop's black front above black awning: ARTISAN PARFUMEUR in round gold script. Repeated in smaller letters. On front overhanging edge of awning. Ditto for dress store next door. Word COUTURE on little black awning fringe. COUTURE VOLPY repeated on shop window. To left of that—arched portico with trim of cement grapevines winding out of pots. Gargoyle over door. Next to that CUISINES . . . GENET. Writ large and square. Over enormous display window. Lit from within by brilliant copper counters. Likely lack of neon. Making one think signs practically absent. Earlier.

Letter from young friend Z chez nous. Saying she glad I found my dream café.

40. Also lying by writing day forty. Because sometimes no entries for ages. Or several in a sitting. Could name them after calendar of French Revolution. 9 *Fructidor,* harvest. 12 *Brumaire,* autumn mists. 18 *Thermidor,* resistance/intransigence. Which calendar based on multiples of ten. This being "rational." So day of rest every ten instead of every seven. Proving ultimately too much. Even for hardworking French. Like all of us wanting their sabbatical. Why not *Thermidor.* Ad infinitum. For us the generation that lost. 9 Thermidor. 900 Thermidor. 20,010. Thermidor being always with us. In meaning of obstacle or stagnation. Of Revolutionary principles. Leading to sentimental brackishness. In French Revolution. Then Russian. Then post May '68.

Dear Z: Visit yesterday to Carnavalet. Museum of French Revolution (so you don't think I'm only sitting in cafés). Each brocaded curtained period room opening on another. Around similarly interlocking gardens. From where Madame de Sévigné earlier wrote her letters. To her beloved daughter. Mocking fellow nobles. The King arrived Thursday evening; the hunt, lanterns, a full moon, a stroll, a light meal on a carpet of jonquils. The roast lacked at a few tables. Meanwhile—an old woman going out rue de Sévigné exit. Getting purse grabbed so hard. Falling. And breaking her nose.

It was about to rain. I saw the sky suddenly darkening through the open window. Further reflected in glass doors of Second Empire cabinets. Shelves flagging objects projecting images of bloody exuberance. Sèvres saucer with man waving Marie-Antoinette's head. Man on plate gleefully collecting blood in basin. Gushing from guillotined neck. Citizen Le Sueur's watercoloured cut-outs of citoyens and citoyennes: patriotic women's club snug in bonnets. Marat on shoulders of supporters. Revolutionary army: sans culottes: apprentice butchers. Hunters. Citizens with placards: *Vivre Libre Ou Mourir,* Freedom or Death. Pasted in little groupings on deep blue sky. Hard flat edges. Precursing social realism. In succeeding rooms: succeeding revolutionary waves. Checked by defeat or Thermidor. When populace taking comfort in cosy interiors. Before hopeful ordinary people again building better barricades than ever. In defence of phantasmagoria of bourgeois-worker brotherhood. Why shouldn't they—prefect sniffing. They've no fortunes to compromise. Leading up to Commune. Exposed offhandedly. In long narrow alcove. A few objects including plate for printing "*L'Internationale.*" Plus painting of a pair of nice fat Paris rats. Communards eating during siege. In front of which straggling group of socialist ladies from Provence. Clucking embarrassed.

Sympathetic. More gold-leafed drawing rooms. Wherein decades of struggle ending—under Bonaparte.

Also ending in Proust's bedroom. On Haussmann's boulevard. Lined with cork so hearing not a thing. Large bed. At end of which a desk. Rolltop if memory serves. Lovely black upholstered

43

chaise longue. Plus armchair. Would it have changed his way of writing. Had Commune won. Would he have still received an invitation embossed with art-nouveau flowers. By Dufy. To the *One Thousand and Second Night* party. Would he still have eaten Camembert. Le fromage qui marche. Round in the evening. Fleeing in the morning. Like Paris itself.

Why not.

Leaving museum by rue des Francs-Bourgeois. Named for hostel of bourgeois. In early 17th—still too poor to tax. Stepping into Jewish/gay quarter. Clouds parting above the ancient buildings. Revealing piece of bold blue sky. Shaped like an eye. In memory's inexplicable way—eyeing self as girl. Your age. Possibly a virgin. Hitchhiking along road by rivière l'Isère. At foot of Alps. As we walking my period overflowing. On fresh white jeans. We getting picked up by a couple. The wife terrified of his driving. Nagging him. Totally hysterical. They inviting us for drink. We are offered some kind of sherry. Sitting there sipping. Looking down at lovely green hills. I open my knees. So he can see the spot.

Why?

41. The men's clothing window across the street. Now having a geometric green chair shaped like a Z. In profile and standing on its edge. As if leaning forward uncomfortably. On tips of its toes. Among neat diagonal rows of shiny shoes. Adjoining display window showing only a patchwork jacket lying on its back. Announcing colours bright and clown-like this autumn. Continuing theme of poverty in fashion. Patches of brute silk. Linen burlap. Hemmed unevenly at bottom. Sack-style purses. Objects glowing magically. With more than monetary value. E.g. when wood becoming table. It standing—euphemistically—on head. Before other merchandise. Abandoning itself to caprices more bizarre. Than if it were to dance. To paraphrase B. Paraphrasing Marx. Surrealists understanding this exquisitely. Using found objects for experiments. Of which exchange value long since diminished. Leaving only magic. Of aura.

The magic I trying to collect. Is again the wildly optimistic yet heartbreaking golden blue. Of early autumn. Sitting in green air of Luxembourg. Thinking if surviving Paris pollution. It due to coming here. Leaning forward on chair. By green-painted glassed-in gazebo. Over apple tart with heavenly almond cream filling. Waving off wasps. It being Sunday. Not just leisure crowd from faubourg. Leading toddlers in starched Edwardian-style dresses. But people from everywhere. Including "the south." More clean and pressed (hopeful). Than anyone. Sitting round tables. Chatting. Reading papers.

I opening yesterday's *Le Monde*. Caricature of Interior Minister Pasqua. Waving off briefcase. With French Constitution in it. Using precisely same annoyed gesture. As if waving stinging buzzing creatures. Off almond cream tart. Cartoon caption saying: *Débarrassez-moi de ça*, rid me of this. The Constitutional Council having declared his proposed changes to immigration statutes. Aimed at preserving homogenous face of republic. As being contrary to Human Rights. Just then woman in sari. Leaping up and wildly waving at ear with both hands. "One" *momentarily* thinking: she likely having worse than wasps to contend with. At home.

Then: but what if she from here . . . . . . . . . . . . . . . . . . . . . .
. . . . . . . . . . . . . . . . . . . . . . . . . . . . . . . . . . . . . . . .

At next table Frenchman eating with American family. Only men talking. How do you say hello American asking. Then losing interest. Subject changing to cost of social benefits for employees. French companies paying thirty per cent. American not knowing how much chez eux. But thinking not much. Or else woulda noticed. Making note to ask his accountant.

Still lovely whimsical day. Even if iron table wiggling. Unsteadily. On sandy ground. Tennis balls a-clacking. At a nearby table young man. Black curly hair. Rather puffy eyes. Gazing nostalgically in distance. Daughter beside him. Tender. Complicit. He reaching over and brushing crumb off her face. To round out increasingly problematic picture. Pigeon limping by with broken foot.

41 *bis*. Now dreaming I a white-draped statue. No pupils. Like that madwoman seen again the other day. On way to Edgar-Quinet. Looking at me directly. Iris floating up. Terrifying effect. Likely just trying to focus. Dream-statue possibly implying I sexless. Been so long. Doing it would be like climbing over wall. Almost unscalable. Unless dream due to having read du Camp's fake anthem to flâneur. Before falling asleep:

> *Love frightens me too much; I don't want to love.*
> *Walk then! walk! you poor piece of misery,*
> *Take your sad road and pursue your sad designs.*

42. P calling. Saying faubourg bad influence. Saying meet her at place des Fêtes. Heart of old Belleville. Working-people's neighbourhood. This after troubling dream in which she pregnant. Therefore having to pee all the time. Old Belleville, c'est fini. S warning on phone. Meaning huge square. Former open-air site of great popular balls, guinguettes. Frequented by old socialists. Commemorating Commune, etc. Replaced by shopping mall.

But it being Sunday—mall completely empty. Wind gusting over cement. Over deserted drafty boulevards. Though climbing up little butte, ridge—nice rows of porous brick cottages. On little curving streets. Named LIBERTÉ. ÉGALITÉ. FRATERNITÉ. Street likewise empty. Save one hysterical woman. Whose white Renault being towed for parking. Other women in African garb coming home from church. Very sympathetic. Lower down man on grey corner. Selling tickets for "magicians in métro."

We entering café opposite art-nouveau entrance. For parc des Buttes-Chaumont. Kind of wrought-iron praying mantis. Delicately sniffing sideways. In banner of vines and floral patterns. The park—former huge Paris refuse heap. Looking over gallows. Its mountain-like mounds. Ravines. Housing terrible rat population. Now seeming all green and grassy. From window of painted plywood café. With chipped formica tabletops. Like chez nous. Fat child serving bitter espresso. Caucasian going by. Face a fold where eye plucked out. Then café door opening. Admitting—real elephant man! Thick features (grey). Gathering toward middle of physiognomy. Wide flattened nose spreading trunk-like towards right. Giant nostrils. Taking off glasses to blow. Lighting a cigarette. Opening his paper.

P and I crossing over to les Buttes. Down green pathways. Over little curved bridges spanning bubbling "cascades." Including Pont-des-Suicides where scores jumping off. Before protective grilles set up. Huge grotto held together by mesh and cement. We climbing high to little lookout temple/gazebo. Fab view of Paris. Faint breeze. Pale green and misty. Magic. I close/protective by P's smooth neck. Appartement de rêves, house of dreams. Aragon calling site. In floating light young man and woman kissing. He suddenly stopping and staring. As if wishing to hit me.

And down below. In this neighbourhood of subjects. Eternally resisting. Being objects. Piaf first appearing. As baby in basket. On somebody's steps. Now restaurants. Boasting best Asian food in West. Plus clubs. Boasting best music. Out of Africa.

43. Walking to tour Eiffel. God only knowing why. Mood blacker by the minute. Above head—Eiffel's iron shadow. Riveted together one century back. By 300 acrobats. Celebrating progress. Slowly gilding in lowering sun.

At shadow's feet. On grassy Champ-de-Mars. Mother. Sticking out foot. To stop little son. When he crawling left. Stopping him with foot when he crawling right. Tearing from eager little hands. Every dead leaf or blade of grass picked up. Child wailing in frustration. Then dropping to knees. Starting over again. Woman a little stout in black skirt and white blouse. Glasses. Glancing each time she cutting him. At adult companion. With certain satisfaction. The howling child's open mouth of frustration. Physiognomy of failed collector. Unable to hold objects. Long enough to place in context of his contemporaneity: mouth. Ear. Diapers: wet. Dry. Smelly. Little collector knowing from experience. Juxtaposing decay (shit) on bubbly new (dewy baby lip). Breaking down linear rigidity of perception. Mother trying to reinforce.

Retreating down street. Named after general. Passing divine art-nouveau glass-petal canopy. Its little glass fingers spreading. Over portico of apartment. Down long hot autumn street. Exclusively Third Republic (i.e. stuck-in-19th ambience). Crossing deserted gigantic Napoleonic parade ground. Esplanade des Invalides. When from esplanade's line-up of silver lindens. Statuesque woman emerging. Red red lips on creamy skin. Otherwise all silver. Silver tailored suit. Long silver pageboy. Little laced boots. We eyeing each other for minute. Five layers of gold leaf on Napoléon's dome. Glowing in rear. Before she ringing embassy doorbell. Reminding me to charm. Requiring anecdotes.

Speaking of anecdotes: back in studio. Reading in paper. About theatre in one of those little caves or grottos on quay walls or in bridge buttresses. Over Seine. Run by homeless monologuist Casquette. Smallest hidden theatre in Paris. Bars of tiny opening having been loosened. Planks brought in. For sitting. Candles. Ladder for spectators to climb up. Then crawling in on stomach. At appropriate moment turning sideways. For fitting embonpoint. Through tiny opening. Suffocating odour. On this particular evening Casquette's ruddy buddy Jean-Claude. Playing God. Unfortunately forgetting lines. So when "dying" Casquette saying: *Father I wish to give a gift to the Holy Church in recompense for my sins. To whom do I make the cheque?*—Silence——Casquette's now corpse finally prompting J-C in stage whisper—*To the Holy Ghost Bank!* Sometimes they joined by popular theatre professionals. The '70s aesthetic being resuscitated in '90s. Which professionals now off in Avignon. Will they return. Will Casquette's London girlfriend Tamara. Eighteen. Having come. Because reform school saying Paris bad. Now gone back. Or Fildoche. Who when high dropping crutches. Climbing quay walls. Recently carried in Casquette's arms to hospital.

I knowing I must go there. Though claustrophobic even in métro. Otherwise missing Paris I expecting. Then phone ringing. C saying incredibly she knowing that guy Casquette. Who often drinking in café near pont Louis-Philippe. With tiny ornate winding staircase to premier étage. Where she going late at night. After writing. Devouring spiced sausage. Lentils. Served on thin marbletop tables. Wrought-iron legs. Or drinking with café's Auvergnat proprietors. Casquette being one of characters of neighbourhood. Coming in nightly off quays.

I nearly asking. Again. If her mother would be jealous.

44. Sun. It being Thursday. Concierge ringing bell. Too early. I pretending to be up. By wearing tights to bed. Just having to throw silk shirt over. To appear in lounging outfit. When answering. She delivering letter. From nearly bankrupt publisher. Saying projected little Bk of Murder'd Wom'n. Potential hangover. Too theoretical. Plus lacking anecdotes.

Depression passing immediately. In raising store on yet another yellow-gold autumn day. Then crawling back between squiggly black-and-white sheets. First making coffee. On radio soft elegant woman's voice saying *France-Musique*. Then piano. Violin. Slipping back to dream. B saying threshold between dreaming and waking: ideal site for projecting past (dream). Into present (real). And reverse. Producing. Through shock of encounter. Spark of illumination. Which dialectic movement. Actually deep kernel. Of montage history method. Unfortunately my dream narrative inadequate. Being only that I am to be married. To a MAN! Much younger. Wealthy. Very smooth black hair. I lacking right clothes. His family paying for black silk dress. Tailored. And stockings.

Mother in background. Can't tell if egging me on. Or sad because I marrying a Catholic. Anyway. Doing it willingly. Not dwelling on nagging feeling that *me-ning*—that's how word appearing—has slipped.

45. Being stood up at la Coupole, Bar Américain. Like being stood up at OK Corral. Rush of relief. Contentedly reduced. To examining black-and-white geometric pattern. Of checkerboard bar floor. As if Diaghilev stage set. Some paunchy gentlemen in suits. Conversing in Russian. Elderly Montparnasse ladies. Dyed hair.

Thin at crown. Due to pollution. Shoulder pads under fine woven dresses. Pouring tea from white round pots. Into cups emblazoned with Modern Style women. Bobbed hair in profile. B saying lesbian Modern Style. In her *sterility*. Unfortunate choice of words. Bar also boasting American-style air conditioning. Freezing. Downstairs. Washrooms comfortable as living rooms. Instead of usual café tiny unisex unit. I warming hands on cup.

Ordering another.

Perhaps I have a fever. The whole day starting wrong. In kitchen (naked) making coffee at 9. The concierge passing—hearing. Shouting through steel reinforced door.—Oh you're up! I'll bring your mail. So instead of crawling back beneath covers. With cup. To read B on subject of various Paris spectres. George Sand dressed as man riding a horse across city. Accompanied by Lamartine. Dressed as woman. . . I dressing. Tidying quickly. So when she handing in mail. Simultaneously looking over shoulder with quick left and right movement of head. Won't see appalling mess. I even raising up outer store or shutter. To signal I on feet.

Then she never coming.

Outside—tomorrow's spectres passing. Women from everywhere. Dressed in black. Accessorized with leopard in capes. White faux-leather bombers. Studded belts. Depending on origin. Stepping over dark roses. Left in lee of parked motorcycle. For funeral opposite. I stepping—still freezing—onto already shadowy roaring boulevard Montparnasse. Racing to Luxembourg. To soak up what's left of sun. It being Sunday. Frenchmen of all ages. Walking loves of their lives: mothers. In oversized hats. Sons leaning courteously. Smiling vaguely. Past homeless individuals. In layers of skirts or jackets. Widows playing bowls. Maids pushing prams. Hemingway crossing this park. Pram full of belongings. Bawling eyes out. Hadley having dumped him. For sinning. (Which was why he coming in first place.)

But why that alpine-looking woman S wanting me to meet. Not showing up. Deciding to find out. Re-crossing Montparnasse. Down rue de l'Ouest. S's inner courtyard. Gleaming wooden stairs.

Smelling of lemon polish. Like all well-kept French apartments. They claiming they expecting me. S's bachelor pad. Totally transformed. Flowers everywhere. Making it light and airy. Bachmann line on window. *Sur la terre comme au ciel.* Orange paper covering table. Plateau with cantaloupe. Watermelon. Bright pink shrimp. Radishes. Rice and chicken dish. Surrounded by sautéed bright red peppers. Women leaning back smoking. Listening to songs from Siberia. Rollicking Russian music. One. Voice of woman prisoner. Not missing husband back home. Because fiancée's a pretty little woman. A treasure. *Filling my mug with rotgut. Instead of red caviar. "He"'ll paint my bread with lipstick.* Gazing affectionately at S's dark bangs. Pristine profile of Alpine-looking woman. German anarchist in rimless glasses. Lipstick dyke in fez. Brushcutted prof with fab job. Reading successive manuscripts. Of famous women writers. Then constructing narrative of process. Which narrative she calling materialist criticism. Watching. I thinking: My Women of the Left Bank.

Raining in Sarajevo.


46. Almost noon. Delicious African-French woman on TV saying. Cool and windy. Tips of her magnificent black waves tinted gold. Undulating. Smiling sunnily. Saying look at it this way. Bad weather's advantageous. Saying it blows off pollution. Smiling. Smiling. The blond-tinted waves announcing the right amount of artifice.

I giving up trying to knot scarf à la parisienne. Deciding to eat in bistro. Minor wallet transgression of omelette. While lusting after cardinal one of rare steak. With hot mustard. Frites. Saint-Germain abuzz. Bent faubourg man with young Asian au pair. Who leading him by string. For afternoon collation, drink. I choosing seat. In little mirrored alcove. Usual composing of physiognomy. Seeking anonymity. Then rosy Breton waitress bursting out. As I ordering vi-h-n, wine: O la petite cousine québécoise, the little Québec cousin. Conjuring film documentary. Seen recently on TV. Men trapping. Ice-fishing with raccoon-tail hats. Though August.

Opening Breton's *Nadja*. I concealing overly romantic prewar-style cover drawing. Of woman's hand. With woman's head coming out. By wrapping in menu. Not to appear naïve.

47. Dear Z: If yesterday were a dream—could call it *Trois Anglais sur le continent,* three anglo girls abroad (Mother being Protestant). In bed as usual thinking. If one didn't stop for lunch. If one could have lunch served. If one didn't have to take time to clean up after. One's workdays would be infinitely more efficient. As they would if getting up earlier. When phone ringing. P's voice. Laughing. Proposing picnic at Versailles. With her mother. Possibly a spy.

Grey and windy. Train leaving enclave. Dipping into tunnel. Under ugly suburbs. Just as very threatening bum. Sitting down beside us. P's mother pulling out album of ancestors. Sitting cradling rifles. Behind several gorgeous dead tigers. With thoughtful velvet muzzles. Somewhere in India. But mostly I remembering. Our astonishment. Mounting broad broad alley. At hugeness of rosé-hued palace. Wide as city block. Glinting real gold. On parapets and railings. Alive with stone figures. Waving irrepressibly. Holding mirrors. Horns of plenty. Raised. Swords. Shields. Torsos twisting this way and that. Leaning back. Or forward. In direction of Sun King's golden face. Which French gaiety. Translating into sex and anarchy. Of (later) revolutions. According to B.

Les trois Anglaises proceeding. Bemused. On tiptoe as in a minuet. Little twirling sandstorms blowing up from pathways and alleys. Between geometric gardens. Emanating from shimmering palatial centre. P claiming fresh varieties of flowers. Formerly popping up each morning. Pushed from maze of tunnels under. By hidden gardeners' hands. Running on laughing. Past cone-trimmed hedges. Artificial lakes. Canals. Blue forests. Seeking place to picnic. No sooner sitting on nice patch of lawn. Then whistled off by cop. I saying let's not provoke them. In case they asking for visa. P's mother incredulous. My dear you just smile sweetly. I've crossed many borders. Without any papers.

We finally opening bread. Sausage. Wine. Chocolate. Near grounds' outer wall in long unkempt grass. Intercut with ha-has. In distance group of tourists. Waiting for les Eaux Magiques to spurt. In many colours. From chariot of Apollo. AKA Louis XIV. Half-immersed in pond. Très beau S saying. Enfin—faint Wagnerian music. And huge jets of water. Aided by naughty wind. Instead of dancing artfully over Apollonian charabanc. Pursuing tourists. Fleeing this way and that. Les trois anglaises laughing. Laughing. In long grass near ha-ha.

Then down hilly road. Past some men pissing in the wind. P running ahead. Obviously in tears. Castle high behind. Hall of Mirrors likely reflecting us. Ambling through rustic hills and vales. Shimmering green and blue. Over horizon. Marie-Antoinette's hamlet. Little curved bridgelets. Thatched roofs. Like operatic set. Inspired by Rousseau. Where queen playing at being simple. *Watching* the haying. From her little gallery. Where sheep still grazing contentedly. Where little creeks still gurgling. Flowers growing wild. We anglaises finding this ambience progressive.

But why P so triste. Over espresso in small Simenon-type café. Back at end of alley. Scuzzy Turkish toilet. A kind of rage flickering. Across her dusky cheeks. Around us families eating Sunday dinner. Agneau/flagelets, lamb/flagelets. Ris-de-veau, sweetbreads. Brochet, pike. Racket from balcony above. People celebrating something. In linen scarves and high heels. Drinking cocktails. Tri-colours.

Back in studio. Watching *Reds*. Depressing film about horrible defeat of American left.

48. Still flummoxed by that extravaganza yesterday. S claiming beautiful. Calling C to ask how she—*100 per cent* North-American French—perceiving Versailles. Not home. Putting on leather jacket. Going to sit in park at Sèvres-Babylone. In shadow of pricey Bon Marché's pointed-helmet domes. By architect Eiffel. Next to blue-tailored woman. Studiously gazing over heads of Arab-French children. On green bench opposite. Woman's shoes. Coat. Hair.

Perfect to point of impossible. Contemporaneous version of those bouffant-clad ladies. Abandoning passages, arcades. Latter 1800s. Rushing to contemplate mass-produced products. In new department stores. Along post-Commune boulevards. Suede heels with straps. Riding skirts. Kick pleats. Jabots. Little silk braided whips. It being reassuring. After all those revolutions. To feel part of crowd. Below: sandbox. Squeals of starched, French children. Nannies from everywhere. Suddenly elderly bourgeoise beside me. Snatching up her purse. Having noticed large patch starting to tear open. On flapper-type band. Along bottom of my leather jacket.

I sitting on. Wondering if gaze. Like at the movies. Altered by company. Time passing in stiff little clouds. Whipping across sky. Little blue eyes. Instantly becoming their opposites. Blinking. Self-displacing. To left. Then to right. Suddenly aware that statue-eyed woman. With pupils disappearing under upper lids. Now on bench opposite. Where Arab-French children sitting before. Usual neat cheap blazer. Cloth shoes. "Gazing" right at me. Young male with red brushcut and greasy suede jacket. Sitting close beside her. Arm around his sweetheart. Also smirking in my direction. Is it her entirely white gaze. Head so high with effort of seeing. Making her seem bold and fearless. Frightening "one" a little.

Turning head vaguely. Beyond trees: turning plaque of old-fashioned round kiosque on corner. Advertising Paris newspapers. Little man standing all day within. Chatting. Chatting. Eyes as bright as sparrows'. Red blotches on face. From toxic waste in air. Or some contemporary plague. Wondering how Gertrude Stein making picture of you sitting there. In portrait of about three words. First getting picture of you as individuals. Then changing. Until she getting picture. Of you as a whole. Without losing something.

## 49. *"Acid Apotheosis"*

Vitrines of chic men's clothing boutique. Opposite. Changed again. So chair shaped like Z. Turned around and on its toes. No longer poised between diagonal rows of very shiny men's shoes. In middle window. But in window on the right. Albeit still precariously on "toes." With a standing stuffed brown suit. "Leaning" paper "hand" on chair's "back." Suit cut wide in legs and jacket. Casual to point of slumming. Yet suitable for boardroom. In window on left—now sitting a tiny house on bed of straw. Eyes running over three tableaux again. House. Shoes. Stuffed suit. Do they add up to a narrative.

By now almost cloudy. Drawing "one" ironically. Like shavings on a magnet. Heading down du Bac. Passing eternal grey façades of 18th/19th buildings. Word ennui again. Gates closed over green hidden courtyards. Paris's unconscious. Turning corner. Crossing pont Royal. Grey brown light exuded by Seine. The air of Paris. A republican notion. Some poet saying. Faint smell of pollution. Baudelaire revelling in presenting his Paris as appearing out of mist.

Cutting towards narrow streets of old Jewish quarter. To meet H-the-anarchist. Plus Alpine-looking woman. Who earlier not showing up. At Coupole. Cloudy but not foggy. Storefronts conjuring Jewish neighbourhood. Chez nous. Yellow. Turquoise. Mosaic tiles. Pastry shops and delicatessens. Familiar smoked meat. Chopped liver. Poppy-seed pastries. Script-shaped eight-branched Hanukkah candelabra. Old red-cardboard bound notebooks. Yellowed pages with turquoise graph patterns. I buying one. H buying rest. Small fair hand grasping one then another. With French francs translated from healthy German marks. Of fat unemployment stipend. Ludicrously I jealous.

Streets so narrow. Walking single file along tiny sidewalks. French woman—Simone-de-Beauvoir clone—in twisted-back hair and '40s-style skirt. Near façade with ring-nosed oxen heads. Shouting after us. Have you seen a mailbox. Have you seen the post office. Have you seen the treachery of the government. Of ministers. Walking. Walking. Ultimately entering old passage Vivienne. Renovated to haute luxe: gleaming brass lampholders. In military rows. Waxed uncracked marble floor. Coming toward us under shining glass dome. Two African-French brothers. Aged roughly five and six. In grey flannel shorts and fine French sweaters. Leaning on each other. One with "darky-face" on cap. Big red lips over cap visor. Holding large cigar. Marching smiling. As if to some internal rhythm. Conscious of effect.

Out rue des Petits-Champs exit. Right to women's bar. Door opening and girl in silk bomber. Jeans. Heels. Coming out. Climbing into sportscar. Malheureusement H refusing to go in. Silhouettes of males being visible. Through blue tinted glass. So turning back again. Walking. Walking. Repassing façade with two ring-nosed heads of oxen on it. Carved message under: DE CETTE ÉCOLE, 165 ENFANTS FURENT DÉPORTÉS EN ALLEMAGNE PENDANT LA DEUXIÈME GUERRE MONDIALE, ET EXTERMINÉS DANS LES CAMPS NAZIS, from this school 165 students were deported to Germany during the Second World War, and exterminated in Nazi camps. Poem painted across neighbouring delicatessen window. *You can sow my ashes / On the four corners of imbecility / No one will silence me.* We devouring plates of liver paste. Marinated vegetables. Delicious bread. Cold white wine. Possibly to provoke. Due to disappointment about women's bar. I starting raving to these women "separatists." On subject of hysteria. Citing Victor Hugo's daughter Adèle. Wandering over oceans and continents. Allegedly after some young British officer. A search I insisting—fork in the air—for something else entirely. Two pairs of blue eyes. Watching me intensely.

50. Waking feeling empty. Then tedium vitae. Providing axis B saying. On which turning old wheels of melancholy. Falling back asleep. Dreaming Holmes by the fire. Nineteenth-century subject. Cosy. Contained. Yes. This is what "one" missing. Earlier looking out at little house on straw. In left vitrine across street. Seeing it for a divine small silver rabbit. At store closing they letting out to run around display space. His shit small and tight. Like mine. The shit turns black from soot.

Pulling on jeans. Black sweater. Jacket. Outside cool and windy. Half-running out. Towards la Coupole. Nose running copiously. To appropriate one of those menus with checkerboard logo. Conjuring stage sets. Of Russian expatriate Diaghilev. Who among first to bring time into 20th. I.e. rendering it disjunctive. By lengthening dancer profiles. Into giant shadows. Or subjects. While choreography (gestures). Hachured. Kinetic machines. Like cube-faces. Of landscape. Flowing in fake line of continuity. Past window. Of Gertrude Stein's automobile. But just as I slipping menu into bag. Waiter grabbing it. As if all foreigners. Behaving same.

Maybe mistake to come. Air conditioning so strong it taking two coffees. First. Express. Second. Au lait. To stay warm. Watching dowagers in dyed hair and shoulder pads. Bantering with waiters. Walking home to studio. Thinking growing old in Paris. Maybe nice. City being circular. Métro. Every half-kilometer. Provided "one" having money for apartment. Even great Baudelaire. Fort éprouvé par la maladie, sick. Shuffling from pension to pension. At end of days. Miming—with sarcasm of despair—post-Revolutionary hailings. Between citizens. Who *en principe* on equal footing. Therefore each saying bonjour Monsieur. Bonjour Madame. To other. Though bourgeois squeezing worker. Increasingly. Toward periphery.

In absence of fire—turning on TV. Fourteen families from "south." Expelled from Montparnasse squat. Sent to hotel. For two weeks only. After which—————————. Then extreme right leader Le Pen. Plus gaggle of followers. Singing nationalist song. Hands on hearts. Somewhere en Provence. Turning off again. Opening B to see again how he conjuncting dream-time (nostalgia). With contemporaneous. Volume falling open at section on dream houses. In which he juxtaposing Le Corbusier's light airy abode. Minimalist interior. Looking out on highway. On small-windowed-turned-in-on-self overstuffed Victorian home.

B adding:

*Que les choses continuent comme avant: voilà la catastrophe.*
I taping it to TV screen.

50 *bis*. This morning—Sunday—someone coming and taking the little rabbit out of cage. In display window across street. It running happily around. Because no one staring at it through pane. Or else used to new context of captivity. However—rabbit house now gone. Single pair of shoes sitting. Where house sat before.

51. Today feeling better. Sky clear azure. Which transparency Baudelaire hating. Preferring clouds nudging each other. Exchanging winks. Conjuring up eyes of queen of poet's heart. Among "that crowd of demons." Causing Flaubert to write: *You Baud are detached from the flesh*. Which detachment Flaub naturellement finding endearing.

Sky growing paler. Thinking of walking to canal de l'Ourcq. On outskirts. Where Baud liking to stroll. But walking there taking hours. Or if using métro. Losing some of precious sun. Still shining down invitingly. Sinking earlier and earlier. Behind grey buildings. Instead—drifting east on Saint-Germain. Past Italian suit at bus stop. Showing father in peaked cap of peasant. How coloured stripes of Paris buses. Announcing destination. Past BRASSERIE LIPP. Menu still saucisses, sausage. Parisian-fried potatoes. In their parsley. As when Hemingway dining there. On *Toronto Star* articles. Thanks to high currency. Past CAFÉ DE FLORE. Where Sartre smoking cigarettes. Ca 1950. More optimistic clouds. Over clothing stores. Books. Markets. Fruits. Vegetables and flowers. Of Saint-Germain-des-Prés. Plus raisin brioches. Heavy with butter. Providing '60s new-wave film ambience. To where boulevard curving to Seine. Faint smell of mint tea from courtyard of INSTITUT DU MONDE ARABE.

It being late as usual. Not taking glass elevator up. To high terrasse. To see how contemporaneous Arabia's glass-and-steel architectural statement. Dialoguing with Notre-Dame Gothic. On opposite side of Seine. Albeit accidentally sidetracking. Into Institut library. No bag-checks in or out. Which trust amazing. Given Arab-French citizens. Hassled regularly in Paris. Also walking right by Institut's featured exhibition. Of modern Arab furniture design.

Instead taking steel set of stairs. To sub-basement. Surrounded by Caucasians. To see *Egypt Photographed by 19th-Century Europeans.* I.e. to see how "we" formerly seeing "them." Small yellow photos. High Egyptian skies. Casting glowing light like melted silver. As Flaubert writing mother on first glimpsing "Orient." Every grouping or landscape image embossed with photographer's unconscious. The Greek—from island nation—focusing on shiny water. Nile boats. Bridges. Water buffalo. The Italian—hard-edged close-ups of men. Working. Lounging. With tools. Conjuring later neo-realist cinema. The Frenchman composing portraits in rather formal groups. Tone somehow ironic. Turk specializing in intimate shots of family and women.

Wonderful exhibition! I grinning. Buying postcards. Trying to be friendly. To cashier in museum boutique. He staring scornfully.

As antidote—café crème on terrasse. Opposite. In shadow of Institute's arabesque patterned walls. Steel panels. Cut out in middle. Delineating glass petals. Containing thousands of photoelectric cells. Miming traditional moucharabieh manner. Of sifting out or letting in light. Pale cloud-streaked sky. Rapidly thickening overhead. Young waiter's brilliantined cranium. Bending to ask after elderly woman client's health. Smiling obsequiously above her. To show he nice. Not great she replying. And yours.

Tapant la balle comme d'habitude, marking time (bouncing ball) as usual.

Now to find a bus.

Attendre c'est la vie, living is waiting.


52. *"Attendre, c'est la vie."*

In warm Paris evening. I waiting on steps of Opéra-Bastille. Among haunted eyes of countless multinational wanderers. Avoiding thinking. Of that guy pushing in. As I going out coded locked door of building. On way over here. He wearing peaked cap like they wearing in Brecht plays. Or dance performances. Calling up heyday of Argentinean tango. From outside I watching him knock for concierge. Now I'm going to get it. She always railing against certain types. Getting into building. Rolling watery baggy eyes. Towards upper storey. Where wealthy Senegalese family living. To my surprise they chatting gravely. Amicably. Maybe he informer with immigration police. Checking up on—someone.

But such a long wait showing lack of respect. Racket phenomenal. Rows and rows of cars. Buses. Whipping around huge traffic circle. With its green July Column. Marking graves of dead insurgents. Buried in ex-basement of fallen Bastille prison. Also on pavement. Some Parisian feminists. Fasting to protest rape as weapon. In ex-Yugoslavia. Sitting on very clean blankets. Plastic water bottles. Young Bosnian. With huge bandage. Over disappeared nose. Standing beside.

Finally S appearing. Around cement corner of ugly modern Opéra-Bastille building. Designed by architect from chez nous. Not alone as I expecting. That lipstick dyke again. Cool. From the suburbs. Dim slanting light. Showing up the down. On her youthful throat. We walking past darkish 18th-century buildings. Across an open space. Sign HÔTEL CLIP. Then into courtyard. As long as a street. Sloping cobblestones. At faucet a woman washing hands. Rinsing out washbasin. No plumbing. As if century earlier. Above her—our party. Dancing by huge picture window. Of shiny renovated coach house. Dilapidated six-storey dwellings. Rising all around.

An L-shaped room. Lesbians on short side. Straights on the long. Gays floating between. Transsexual Catherine. Small nipples visible under burgundy silk shirt. Faint moustache. Dancing cheek-to-cheek with fags. Tall slightly pregnant parisienne. Head thrown back. Black dress over small round stomach. In almost decadent slide across floor. Lovely mezzo climbing urgently. Not to say hysterically. Over lyrics of "Nous sommes des animaux," "we are animals." Song from late 19th salons. White poodle endlessly dry-humping leg of touslehaired guy. In baggy cords. I.e. British. The hostess white African. Serving ham. Pineapple. Taboulé. Cake. Champagne.

On divan. I waiting party out. My cold preventing me. I telling H-the-anarchist. Also sitting there. From socializing. Soft voices. Hustling courteously. Calling up that ad *La Douce France,* sweet France. Advertising sunny produce of Provence. While on TV angry farmers trashing truckloads of white juicy peaches. Protesting some state marketing agreement. Just then the hostess emitting loud note of reproach. Two African men coming through door. And we naughty guests having drunk all the champagne. Leaving none for them.

But we running out. To catch last métro. Behind us in window. Rhythm heating up. Not watered-down "world beat." But real African. Dancers leaning forward. Suddenly excited.

The Paris I missing.

53. Côte d'Azure tans of August fading. Kohl around eyes no longer making whites so startling. Meaning I practically illegal. I.e. soon requiring visa. I thinking. Walking to Edgar-Quinet. Feet in dead leaves. Marvelling how "one" imagining self major end-of-20th writer. Yet entire days passing. Without single word. Trees on meridian strip. Clipped like ears of bulldogs. Brown tinged foliage. They not faring any better from pollution. Than I.

Now sitting nodding. On terrasse. Slight party hangover. Procuring feeling of belonging. Woman with a life. Only disappointment: table pushed right up against sidewalk. In crowd. Instead of back against warm sunny wall. By row of browning potted cedars. Half of them dead. Where guy with marseillais accent. Basking in warmth of my usual table. Handlebar moustache. Blonde girlfriend. Drinking coffee after coffee. Like I. Large flecks of dandruff. On our collars.

Concierge not speaking to me.

54. Looking out earlier. I seeing elderly Caucasian shuffling by. In raincoat. Well-combed head bent forward. In slump of osteoporosis. And as I writing this. Old woman stepping out of door below. Also bent completely forward. *Third* person. With bone shrinking

illness. I seeing today. In this country of cheese eaters! Probably due to long (post)war shortages.

Supper at C's. Oddly conjuring similar era. Of scarcity chez nous. It being creamed salmon. Like both our mothers making. In '50s. From tin. And powdered milk. Identical. In French or in English. In little houses. Beyond outskirts. Of Montréal. Québec. Sauce made of butter (margarine)/flour/onions. Or their juice. Two cups "milk" (C naturellement substituting crème fraîche). Cooked on double boiler. Also sometimes peas. Poured over toast. Snow likely falling. Or—nighthawks. Diving into heartbreaking pink Paris skyline. Beyond C's high terrasse. Accompanied by suitably light Beaujolais. Endless cigarettes. Taking in strange reflective quality. Of the air of Paris. A synthesis of Gothic spires. Flexed domes. Gold leaf. Iron. Glass. Floating like mirages.

C opening Beaujolais number two. While I unwrapping favourite semi-ripe Saint-Marcellin. Cheese. Firm in summer. Shrinking in autumn. Until at height of maturity. Collapsing over musky creamy centre. We sitting silently. Smoking. Eating. Drinking. Sky blushing fuschia. Taking in Arc de Triomphe. Sacré-Coeur. Panthéon. Bouncing off each other. At distance.

I telling C I practically illegal.

She ignoring this completely. Segueing on. To how Paris. Conferring dignity. On intellectual pursuits. Albeit extreme anxiety. Regarding appearance. She personally never leaving room. Without attention to every detail of hygiene. Accentuated with accessories. Not to mention way of walking. Sitting. Speaking. I telling how Madame X laughing. When I asking where to put what we calling *vidange,* garbage. They calling *poubelle.* Chez nous we also saying *oké.* Where they saying *d'accord. Bonjour* where they saying *au revoir.* Further leaving diphthongs slightly open. Inviting. They closing theirs up suavely. So we nasalizing pain, bread. Causing mockery in bakeries. Which rigour in personal presentation—C further speculating—possibly linked to French love of ritual. Citing habit of hailing butcher. Baker. Etc. In predetermined manner. Politesse oblige. Bonjour Madame. Oui

Madame. Non Madame. Merci Madame. Au revoir Madame. I opining (grant it—miming Baudelaire) so-called rituals. Possibly only empty expressions of equality. Left over from early post-Revolutionary period. C segueing on romantically. To French formula for greeting. When encountering neighbour on street. Precise order for asking after health. Dog. Weather. Saying such rituals unthinkable chez nous. Given extremes of climate. Making us always in hurry. Ils ont le temps doux, they having clement weather. Flowers everywhere. She adding. Dreamily.

Instead of rituals. Would have said gestures. But this possibly Protestant way of thinking. Ritual requiring precise repetition. Whereas Protestantism preferring notion of proceeding forward. Rite or repetition considered waste of time. Or boring.

55. Cool and cloudy. Reading in paper about famous Kenyan athlete. Lacking visa like me. Jumping into Seine. To save elderly Frenchman. In act of suiciding. One month later Kenyan receiving *two* letters from préfecture. One citing bravery. The other inviting him. To leave country. *Not like you.* S declaring on phone. Citing little incident. Witnessed in métro. Plump young white American with brushcut. Sitting on bench. Cop walking up. Vos papiers s'il vous plaît, your papers please. He saying. To young African on left. Vos papiers s'il vous plaît. He reiterating. To veiled woman. Carrying baby. On right. Not a word to brushcut.

56. Walking to place des Vosges. On right bank. Paris's loveliest square. On this unbelievably beautiful bright and sunny day. Albeit lot of dust in air. Square series of enclosures. First "one" entering. Rectangle of business and dwellings. Fronted by quadrant of pink brick arcade columns. Marching round façade's four sides. Like tribunal of judges. Some French poet saying. Within which yet another fenced-in inner grassy square. Built by Henri IV for feasts and celebrations. Fence made of spears. Choosing table in barred shadow thereof. And sitting waiting for H. Kind of taking over from S.

Now she coming. Carrying camera. Hair tucked back under little rimmed hat. I admiring white matte skin. Perfumed. Lipsticked. My bangs thank god hiding enraged splotches of forehead eczema. We drinking coffee. Watching sun playing on leaves of park trees. Splaying lights and spear-like shadows. From behind which emerging large blonde woman. Looking rather poor. Suddenly bending to pick up thin tiny girl. Pants pulled down to pee. In suspended squat between two cars. Child's limbs minuscule. Well-suited man passing. Carrying huge bouquet of lilies. Upside down. Nearly as large as himself.

We sitting on. Growing stripes of shadow. Now barring whole square. Table. Face. Leading H to say cops still hassling her. For having interviewed woman. In prison. From one of those anti-government gangs. Called terrorist in Germany. After which the woman sending postcard. From her little cell. Saying come and visit. *I'm always in.*

Shadows also darkening boutiques under arcade roof. Including entryway in corner. To house of Victor Hugo. So great. Large. He casting huge shadow over 19th-century poetry. Even thinking twin towers of Notre-Dame. Standing for H of his initial. Upstairs in museum. Engraving titled *Hugo Ego*. Another titled *My Destiny* (huge wave). Among theatre notices. Family mementoes. Furniture. Photos. Letters. Few traces of daughter Adèle. Of whom he very critical. For fleeing family sanctuary. In pursuit of young British officer. Over many continents. The odd photo. Her fancy writing case. Carved wood. Romantic-style aquarelle of castle in middle. Pen. With which she writing his words. When still functioning as his scribe. Her mother saying: write. You'll eat your eggs later. Unaware her daughter preparing fugue. From he who knowing how to fill every nook and cranny. A nation's memory. With Himself.

H saying she having to go.


57. Some thick lazy clouds. Suddenly parting. Making almond-shaped gap. Lying back on cushion. With second strong coffee. Opening B. At chapter on *L'ennui, éternal retour.* Definition: to be

drugged or in state of waiting. Though not knowing for what. Then someone knocking on door. At first I not answering. Knocking again. Friend R. From Winnipeg. Sticking bespectacled B-like physiognomy through slightly ajar crack. Handing in card. Written on torn graph paper. *Monsieur R a l'honneur de vous annoncer son arrivée à Paris,* Mr. R is pleased to announce his arrival in Paris. *Il vous invite à lui téléphoner,* and invites you to call him. I parting bangs rather vulgarly. Displaying eczema. Wanting to be alone.

Still we lingering for a minute. He showing me some nice kind of huge cheese knife. For use in Paris lovenest. Designed by Philippe Starck. Rather dramatic wide blade. Ending in parabolic curve. Small triangular handle with little supporting members. For lying knife on side. Sharp edge facing comestible. R saying already feeling. How Paris restoring dignity. Through infinite grace of surroundings. Then off to Starck's citation modern-style café. With its dark ever-widening stairs. Leading to giant clock. On second-storey balcony. To drink coffee in thin white porcelain cups. Maybe that Slavic-looking woman there. I once seeing against brown wall. Writing in notebook.

Retreating to cushion. Noticing. In shop window opposite— rabbit cage BACK. But crowded into corner. By suit. Sitting on mahogany bench. Uncharacteristically cluttering up display. Normally characterized by "stark" simplicity.

Raining in Bosnia.


58. Perfect autumn late afternoon. Thinking of going to Luxembourg. When phone ringing. P in the hospital!

Leaving studio a mess. Bus east on Saint-Germain. Past INSTITUT DU MONDE ARABE. Past JARDIN DES PLANTES. Where she often visiting animals in antiquated installations. Her elegant nose. Plus forehead with brushcut. Peeking through bars. Past GARE D'AUSTERLITZ. Where people arriving from "south." Past derelict in parking lot. Folded forward painfully on cement. Plus portly well-pressed type. Lying flat on back. Neat buttoned coat. Over high hump of stomach. Drunk or heart attack. Through white arch into HÔPITAL LA SALPÊTRIÈRE. Site of Charcot's eager sketches of twisted hysterics. Through octagonal domed chapel. Eerily stripped and empty. Save odd bare wooden statue. Church containing several separate naves. Chairs on diagonal. To keep fools. Prisoners. Women. From eyeing each other. Entering vast green inner park. People mostly from "the south." Strolling to and fro. Low barracks dotting compound. La Salpêtrière, gunpowder factory. Cum prison. Cum asylum. Cum public hospital. In rooms of which— birds now singing through the open windows.

P asleep in her bed. Dusky pink cheeks—still alarming shade of grey. Having received transfusion. Adorable pyjamas with hearts. Ear piercings. Making her look vulnerable. Incongruously I recalling they putting saltpeter in milk. At girls' schools chez nous. To keep libido down. Then wondering if behind innocent closed lids— P feeling angry. Being famous for temper. Once climbing ledge. To throw pavé at spurning boyfriend's window. Breeze filling room. Curtains blowing gently. Leaves whispering happily. No one surveying the coming and the going. Suggesting sickness just a pause. In the gaiety. Making hospitals chez nous. Appear like prisons. Prowling corridors. Finally seeing two nurses in walk-up. Drinking coffee.

Rien d'anormal, nothing abnormal. They saying.


59. Yes ennui covering a tear in the surface. The word t_____ hard to write here. Because for true ennui—t_____ must be of collective origin. Not ennui if only mirroring one's private stage set of afflictions. P in hospital. Or gallery of rogues arriving from chez nous. Saying writer. In leisure lottery studio. Getting nowhere.

Squirting on drop of *Poison* by Dior. Primping hair almost '60s bouffant. Descending into métro. On platform guy selling yo-yos. Lighting up when thrown. Sitting with knapsack against vandalized map of Paris. So nothing getting stolen. But nothing major to report. Except lemony smell on neck. Of expensive blonde. Having wasted yet another morning. In expectation of large French publisher. Calling re: Bk of Md'd Wm'n. Albeit knowing in Paris a promise. Primarily intended to flatter interlocutor.

Waiting. I opening B. To passage explaining how "one." If melancholic 20th persona. As opposed to wily contemporaneous version. Narrating paradox into false line of continuity. Necessarily using ruse to achieve constant state of dreaming (nostalgia). Trick being staying out of light. Which is why solitary travellers. Loiterers. Old sailors in ports. Perpetually at post before dawn. Full of maxims to protect themselves from sun.

Phone in fact ringing once. R calling to report he and friend set up in lovenest. Then having lovely lunch yesterday in Luxembourg. Followed by thé dansant, tea dance. On right bank. Some high glassed-in terrasse. With palm trees. Near Pigalle. R praising the Tintin look of the boys. Little cowlicks or crewcuts. Very sweet faces. Others too muscled. Like they'd be afraid to take their shorts off. In case their pricks had shrivelled. From steroids.

60. Day alternately cloudy and sunny. Leaves blowing on boulevard. Looking closer at display window across street. Seeing standing suit no longer wearing conspicuously striped square garb. Of elegant escroc, thief. But ordinary brown suit. Fine wool. Slightly fitted. Respectable. Except 2 *red paper hands*. Emerging from *each* sleeve. As if bloody from strangling. While in vitrine formerly containing rabbit house. Nothing but stiff white square list of prices. Like a menu. Occasional striped bus. Passing in front. Midnight— *Gare du Nord*. Chocolate—*Opéra*. Azure—*Champ-de-Mars*. Ochre—*Montparnasse*. For hailing at distance.

But I going nowhere. Crawling back between squiggly black-and-white sheets. Re-awaking to huge din below. At first I thinking immigration demonstration. Men from many nations. Marching towards ministry. But it turning out to be soccer. Last night— riots in stands. After skinheads attacking Africans. Followed by misdirected cop brutality. S saying soccer riots here. Having similar significance to hockey riots chez nous. I.e. acting out scenarios. Political in nature. E.g. québécois fans stampeding luxury

Queen Elizabeth Hotel. Ca 1950. After hotel being named for foreign queen on dollars. Instead of local hockey great: Maurice Richard.

Now on TV talk show. Parents of young prisoners. Naturellement mainly mothers. Being interviewed by one of those sympathetic '70s-type "new" French feminists. Permed highlighted bob. Made up. But not too. Seen around Librairie des Femmes. Where I once noticing husband of owner. Between shelves. In box suit of dancer. Shuffling step or two. Of Argentinean tango. Feminist gently squeezing confessions. By expedience of empathy. From guilt-ridden maters. One admitting she homosexual. Hideous blonde wig. Mechanically repeating: it's my fault. I lived with a woman. I never gave my son enough love. Eyes fixed fanatically in distance.

Final escroc note. On *Minitel* (advertising channel): *Work sought: speciality—règlement de comptes,* settling of accounts.


61. Crummy café around corner. Only crummy one in neighbourhood. Crushed mégots, butts on floor. Smoke. Mosaic of broken badly matched beige tiles. Shoes of workers dangling over. Drivers. Cleaners. Gophers. Working for faubourg's high-classed couturiers. Hotels. Restaurants. Making just enough to pay for tiny room.

Rubber-soled shoes. Or pointy cowboy boots. Polished but showing signs of wear. Eye mesmerized by ray of light on beige stucco wall. It occurring to me. Ennui likely bad excuse. For indifference. Therefore pores exuding only *fake* ennui. As smokescreen. For warding off gossipy arrivals. Who saying projected little Bk of MW. Likely dépassé. I resenting their treating work as gossip. R saying au contraire. Gossip an aesthetic. Putting "us" ("homosexuels"). On front burner.

And I glad to say: it raining. Rain coming down straight between the three-to-four-storey walls. Along pale curved street. Outer mirrors. Reflecting inner walls of boutiques. Carefully done in beige or white to catch Paris light. Re-reflected on bent head of woman.

Hair cut with oriental precision. Writing on desk painted same beige as walls. Picking up beige of floor. Vase of the same shade of beige right beside her. Holding almost same colour flowers.

For lunch beige osso buco.


62. Last night crossing Saint-Sulpice. Low-flying pigeons skirting Four Bishops' Fountain. Tiers splashing like incense. Effervescing narrow hotel in corner. Where D Barnes' outrageous doctor. Allegedly holding forth. In silly blond wig. On how Americans hating night. Fog falling faintly. Climbing to tiny second-storey space. Clearly a "scene." Crowded with several unremarkable hats. Certain expatriates still looking for the high times. Having heard in literature departments. Paris belonging to them. Plus a few French anglophiles. With look of enthusiastic strain people getting. Who prefer living in a second language.

Best poet in English! Declaring poet's French translator. Behind huge glasses. Dithyrambically brandishing poet's oeuvre. Declaring such clarté, transparency. Allowing *perfect* rendering. From American to French. C the québécoise. Mole on cheek. Cigarette at ready. Huge brown wink. Indicating we from chez nous knowing a thing or two. About whether any French word. Ever perfectly rendered in English. The poet—almost shaved head. Looking up at audience. As if reading a hieroglyph. Slightly protruding teeth. Nice shiny skin. Some technically fine moments. Some *if-I-just-think-I'm-flying-everybody-will* variety of phrases. People applauding loudly for what running closest to obvious.

Stepping into street. Fog so thick. Barely glimpsing tricorn of H-the-anarchist. Retreating in mist. Other bobbing hats. Appearing here and there. Ambience oneiric. I inching who-knows-where in haze. It seeming prudent to get on bus. Over a hump. Likely crossing Seine. To right bank. Through vast Louvre courtyard. Dim lights of buildings. Bus winding around. Until taped message crooning NOTRE-DAME-DE-LORETTE. In old days bus driver himself crooning little tune. Indicating stops. Deciding to step out. Lost at last in Paris.

Luckily light visible. From butte, hill above. Penetrating fog. Rendering night more transparent. As I climbing cobblestones. Crowded sidewalks of people. Eyeing luscious décolletées for sale. In windows. Increasingly discernible. Or bare backs. Or cascades of demure waves. Adroitly framed in lace curtains. Or shapely legs. Raised on bar stools. Then onto slanting brightly lit Pigalle.

Walking back down. Suddenly feeling happy. When old woman in thick black-and-white sweater. Asking help. For pushing heavy door open. No sooner falling over threshold with effort thereof. When butch bouncer slamming it closed behind. Waving us down worn plush stairs. Entering red-and-black crescent-shaped room. Several lesbians dancing. Average age fifty. Modestly attired. Pantsuits and sweaters. Sweet tired physiognomies. Except one gorgeous young woman. Black curls. Whole bottle of crème de cacao. Plus siphon. Being placed on her table. By bleached blonde management. Simultaneously profiting. By patting her ass. I standing at bar. Other women smiling. Unhassling. In courteous French way. Could easily stay til dawn. Breaking over Pigalle. Bordered on north by abandoned stone building. Pigeons flying in and out of all the empty windows. Under green branches. Leaking gaps of light powder sky. But what if missing last bus. Into street again. Fog completely lifted.

Home by midnight.


63. Waking. Happy. Thinking relationship to Paris. Now one of vague familiarity. Albeit people complaining letters not describing streets. As they used to. Clothes. Façades. In every little detail. I being increasingly caught up. In rhythm of trajectory. As if sentences. Like steps. Driven not by predicates. But by gerund. Or back-and-forth-gesture. Possibly befitting subject. With foreign queen on dollars. E.g. walking down Saint-Germain. Thinking marvellous *surely* to be had. Simultaneously fearing 19th-century buildings. Over shoulder. About to dissolve into dust.

But headache getting worse. Unusual acrid smell of diesel fumes in air. Cloud cover imprisoning pollution. To catastrophic proportions. Causing paleness of physiognomy. Getting up and looking in row of convex mirrors. Face white as museum piece. As in "classical" Parisians. With their jet bangs. Violet eyes. Fente in chin. Possibly constipated. Or expressing some high of sadism. As in Proust's Albertine. Coming to his room. Black satin making her even paler, making her into the ardent pale Parisian languishing from lack of air, from the atmosphere of crowds and perhaps a propensity for vice. I.e. *not* wanting him. Word vice summoning regret. For not staying longer. At women's bar last night.

Raining in Bosnia.

64. Speaking of physiognomy. It is to the realm of memories that the familiar belongs. B again. Tics. Expressions. Rendered familiar through unconscious repetition. Accompanying gestures. Getting up in dark. Anticipatory face looking through cracks in the store. Checking weather. People. Walking down below. Today— woman in white *imper* and white sneakers. White "scottie" on leash. Baguette tight beneath arm. At this hour street still quite deserted. Little ritual. Repeated daily. Opening casement window. While outer store kept closed. Letting in air. Making coffee. Then closing window because traffic racket increasing. Back to bed. Store still down so concierge won't knock. Given her little trick of going out in street. And looking up at window. To see if I on feet. Very pleasant since I giving her 100 francs.

*Her* rituals signalled by position of her curtains. I was going to say routine. Language being precise as mathematics. Gertrude Stein saying. Anyway lace curtains on concierge's glass door. Opening at 8a. Drawn at noon for lunch. Once I knocking then. She appearing pointedly chewing huge chunks of beef. Mouth half open. Beyond pink satin half-curtains. Ten-by-ten room. Total absence of natural light. Curtained-off place for sleeping. Plus kitchenette. From which food and laundry smells floating. Smells so stuffy I feeling nauseous. Particularly with my cold.

Or—one's ritual might be another's routine. Where class or privilege entering. The way she emerging late afternoon. Sitting

71

on green leather sofa in lobby. Listening to radio. Having no one in little loge for talking. Therefore intercepting residents to chat. About certain people not attending daily properly to garbage. Concierges having to get it out wrapped. In green containers every working day but May 1—International Workers' Day. She sympathizing totally. Though disliking immigrants. Allegedly usurping conciergeries all over Paris.

Now in café place de la Bastille. Having glimpsed one more ritual. On way over. Through shutters. Open tiny crack. Revealing little girl. Taking daily after school collation, snack. In street-level flats—shutters almost perpetually closed. For privacy. From eyes of passersby. We both drinking chocolat-chaud. Mine with rich swath of black chocolate across top. Outside—six lanes of noise and pollution. Racing within markers of old Bastille circumference. Around July Column. Over spilled blood of 1,000-plus chopped heads. Here. At Nation. Concorde. Carrousel. Gleeful gestures of assistants. Seen in museum. Collecting blood from blind necks. In laundry tubs. P just on other side. In yellow room. Very clean for entertaining her swain. Neighbours still coughing through wall. TB she repeating. Scrubbing shared bathroom again. A little paranoid like I.

She preferring term guilty.

They both covering fear. I insisting. Watching her hang sheet with yellow roses. On high rack over sink. Fear of retribution. For some past crime committed. But phone ringing. P's pale post-operation physiognomy flushing. Mocking some lover. Which interruption. Letting rise to surface what au fond, at bottom gnawing. From article I reading earlier. Saying fear of failure at certain periods. Can ruin most promising individuals. The Fear of Fear of Failure. Smiling as if a fabulous success. While insides trembling like jelly. Extending to nervousness about shitting in morning. Sitting on toilet heart beating. Tensing up. So nothing happening.

65. Sky growing greyer. Turning on TV. Watching ad for a laxative. Young woman very wholesome. Saying to her older confidante.

*Surely it's not good for me.* We knowing she meaning constipation. Though word never mentioned. The older woman supplying required advice. I.e. product. Camera panning to bridge they standing on. Pristine rivulet. Green rolling landscape. Like Marie-Antoinette's hamlet. Everything as lovely. As misty. As rurally reassuring.

Turning off again. Heading for Pont-Neuf. Hallucinating light. Brown shot with pink. Neo-Situationist slogan: *Rions de notre inconscient,* Let's laugh at our unconscious. Bleeding down buttress. White glow of Seine. Dissimulating Paris's contradictory layers. Wars. Revolutions. Sans-papiers. Murd'd Wom'n. (Shit going elsewhere.) While Grand Palais's magnificent glass dome. Built for 1900 World Exhibition. At bend of river. Still radiating optimism. Of capitalist expansion. Ebony. Silver. Carpets. Ivory. Teak. Brought back from colonies. For reinforcing bourgeois interior. B saying. Against history's boomerang effect.

R and love awaiting. Two corpulent young men. Sitting astride bench. By Henry IV on horse. Le Vert Galant, playboy. Former Protestant. Declaring on conversion. Paris's worth a mass or two. Then stabbed. By religious maniac. Boys gazing into depth of each other's eyes. Seeing perhaps. Also spell of distant illusions. Which spell soon to be enhanced. By infinite pleasures. Of all France's culinary regions. Toulouse potted goose. Marseilles bouillabaisse. Burgundy snails. Caen sweetbreads. Lyon parsleyed ham. Little ripening white cheeses called crottin, droppings. Crème fraîche. Crème brûlée. Crème anglaise. Savorously prepared. By wives of French Communists. For big fête of Communist paper *l'Humanité.*

Capable of lying. I *not* saying (like Baud to his mother):
I wanting to be alone.

Instead—archly plucking cold. From panoply of ailments. Saying *surely it not good for me.* To take métro. Then bus. To La Courneuve. On outskirts. To tramp from tent to tent in mud. Sampling dishes. Even if cooked up. By better halves of France's remaining idealists.

73

Home along quays. Night falling rapidly. Loving this phrase of Baud's:

*Il est plus tard que tu ne crois*, it is later than you think. The *ne* being only *half* a negative. Causing ambiguity. Splitting time in two directions.

Adding it to TV screen.


66. Some evenings. Rather than adrift in Paris. I'm in a television in Paris. Watching bad American thrillers. Or good documentaries. French people remembering. Or drowning in little arty video. Fat woman sucking chocolate from profiterole. On her lips. While husband complaining: you don't understand me. This I passionately absorbing. Head turning as if for a kiss. Or in murmur of agreement. When I turn it off the screen is hot. Magnetic. Energy rising from it. Paper can cling.

I reapplying *Il est plus tard que tu ne crois*. To the surface. When suddenly a shout. At first seemingly in building. Concierge likely screaming at someone. For not answering door. This morning. When she bringing up mail. Consequently preventing her. From visiting dead child in cimetière on outskirts. Given time required. For travelling back and forth on buses. Another shout. Rushing to window. Below. Men under black umbrellas. In dark. As if themselves going to funeral. Maybe in solidarity. With squatting Africans. Thrown out of flats.

Umbrellas a statement.

By time I stepping into jeans. Sweater. Jacket. Then stepping into street. Nothing but mountains of stickers. Declaiming NON AUX LICENCIEMENTS BULL, no to Bull layoffs. Floating down momentarily unemployed boulevard. Almost banally. Everybody knowing. Jobs fleeing to lower-paying countries. In globalizing market. Little charcoal grill with tired sausage smoking. In middle of empty intersection. At Sèvres-Babylone. I following stragglers. Towards new café rue du Bac. LE FLOR. Modest version of famous café *de* Flore. On Saint-Germain-des-Prés. Where Sartre and de Beauvoir. Hanging out. In more optimistic context. NON AUX LICENCIEMENTS

BULL stickers. Plastered over fake-cane backs of plastic chairs. People shouting. Above click and buzz of pinball machines. Elated. Despite odds against them. As if still early '70s. When revolution always seeming. Just around corner. Some even with slightly frizzy look. Left over from era. Stout woman in rather shapeless pants. Standing smoking. At bar. Kind of virile. Blue-collar worker. Maybe one of us girls. I thinking. Then seeing her little man beside her. Kid in his little red cap. And lumberjack boots. Hoisting himself on chair. Watching adolescents. At pinball machine.

Outside café window. Huge bus trying to turn little corner. Small white Renault. Parked too near intersection. Driver backing up and trying. Infinite number of times. While exhausted faces. Mouths half open. Watching from bus windows.

Fax from Z. Chez nous. Saying projected Bk of MW possibly problematic. Because people wanting to be happy.

67. Fax machine ringing. R summoning to dinner. Now impossible to decline. Standing on platform at Sèvres-Babylone. Suddenly spying skinny unaesthetic ass. Jeans pulled up in crack. Of critic friend of R's. Notoriously pro-anecdote. Out at Charenton. Name of Sade's asylum. Heart beating rabbitly. Crossing grassy boulevard strip. Past shop displaying giant seafood platters. All red and yellow. Entering narrow courtyard. Like village. Trees leaning toward each other. In two single rows. Over little mousehole. Escalier D à gauche, stairway D on left. Waxed wooden steps. Smelling usual ultra-citron clean. Concave from use. Door above. Opening into gleaming domestic scene. All shiny white. Plants on window sill. Osterizer. Martini shaker. Soufflé-maker. Apron round N's girth. Dimpled cheeks leaning over parabolic Starck knife. Chopping salade niçoise. R opening rosé. Labyrinthine conversation. Going on between them.

R: Have you lately—N: Ye-e-s—R: It doesn't matter—Me: Don't you guys talk about these things—R: I'm much relieved. The burden of pleasure. Lies not uniquely with me—N: It doesn't matter. I don't want to know what he does—Me: For we girls it often matters very much. We're trying to get over this—N: It doesn't

75

matter—R: Some women feel more powerful than others. For them it matters less—

Conversation then drifting to variations of masculine or feminine. We three. All feeling kind of doubleness. Leading to deviousness of Proust's sentences. Always another twist or turn. Contradictory. Ambivalent. As in way he describing Albertine: . . . *the sweet . . . cheat*. Or—the unpredictability of Sodomites. No sooner they arriving . . . than leaving town again. So as not to have the appearance of belonging. Taking wives. Keeping mistresses in other cities. Where they finding every diversion appealing to them.

Métro home. Via quai de la Gare. Glacière. Remembering. Proust initially self-publishing. Transferring in heart of massive Montparnasse-Bienvenue station. Missing last connection. Maze of abandoned curved tunnels. Abutting onto others. Lights about to dim. Turning. In labyrinth. Walking. Running. Down empty passages. Paris's underpinnings. Curving whitewashed walls. Turning left and right. Lights nearly out. Countless rats allegedly instantly appearing. Gambolling on pavement. Muggers. *At last. . .* Coming to exits. Barred like castle moats. Guy washing floor. Gesturing laconically to last steel-barred keep. Only half descended.

67 *bis*. Fax from summer houseguest. Sending TIPS FOR SUCCESS. She "kind of liking": 1. BE PRO-ACTIVE. Decide what to do. DO IT. 2. THINK OF HOW YOU WANT TO BE REMEMBERED AT YOUR FUNERAL. Balance principles with market prerogatives. 3. FIRST THINGS FIRST. Devote time to what's important. Before it becoming urgent. 4. THINK WIN-WIN. Have abundance mentality. Solutions benefitting all parties benefit you first. 5. BEING UNDERSTANDING PAYS. Don't dive into conversation. Keep eyes open. 6. CO-COMPETE TO COOPERATE. Find ways to seek advantage. While basically pulling together. 7. SHARPEN INCISORS. Continually exercise and renew physical/mental/emotional.

68. Rain. Awake. Head swimming with ideas. Having last night read end of B's *Baudelaire* section. Declaring Poe's lookalike crowd. Trope for dangerous fake or feigned "uniformities." Arising from

certain republican notions of equality. Post-French and -American Revolutions. Getting up. Dressing. Simultaneously discerning through slanting rain. Pale finely woven shirt. Of standing suit. In chic boutique opposite. Now replaced by dark brown corduroy shirt. Indicating fake empathy with labour.

Now really pouring. So not walking over to café on Edgar-Quinet. As planned. Though looking good. Which mattering. In case running into French editor. Claiming to love little Bk of MW. True—woollen leggings a little hot. For season. But with rose turtle-neck. Blousy jacket. Creating nice ligne, silhouette. De rigueur here in fashion. About to be wasted on acrid smoke. Filth. Of crummy café round corner. If rain stopping maybe walking to Pont-Neuf. To take in glass-and-iron roof of Grand Palais again.

Don't know why it getting to me.

Choosing seat in café window. Straight back. Espresso. Served by yellow-with-cirrhosis waiter. Nice blue pen. Graph notebook. Noting how B. In abutting spleen of man (sic) wandering freely in crowd. With exiled anarchist Blanqui's spleen-in-cachot. On Belle-Île. Exorcising sameness. Further—I noting: small white space be-tween facts. And anecdotes. Of montage. Operating break. In spleen of narrating I. When—lightning. Looking up—flash going off again. Woman in red suit with very large camera. Shooting me once more. Then fleeing round curve of rue de Grenelle. Paranoia rising. They definitely after me. Unless case of mistaken identity.

Let them arrest you P laughing. Sitting on table at other end of phone. Long brown neck coming out of heart-dotted pyjamas. Body taut and slender as if still pre-sexual. Like those dancers and spirited women. B calling sisters of Ibsen's. Appearing with inno-cence. Or perversity. Of flowers. On sets of old posters. Along quays. Let them arrest you. Then you'll have something to write about.

69. A lost day.

For some stupid reason eating rabbit twice.

Looking out at window. Across street. Unchanged.

Anyway *two* rabbit courses at potluck dinner. In studio of T. One more compatriot. Arriving via London. In ultra-short modish

77

leather skirt. Bright hennaed hair. Lace stockings. Concierge smiling mockingly. As we stepping arm 'n arm. Through foyer. Though I wanting to be alone. Along quai Voltaire. Over pont au Change. Old money-changing bridge. Right to T's studio. Large. Airy. White. On quiet courtyard side. Two tables placed dramatically opposite each other. On one in middle: Rabbit in cream. The other small and pushed up against windows. Bearing Rabbit in prunes. Also passion flower. Outlined by skies of Paris. Thick with clouds as usual. Nudging each other. Winking. Nuanced. Ambivalent. Like Parisians. I suggesting.

Yeah. To point of no EDGE! T interjecting. Her voice grating high at end of sentence.—Excuse me I saying. *Maybe* things here more complex. *Maybe* notwithstanding certain classical decorum. At least still vestiges of class analysis. In media. Compared to her beloved Britain. Where *edge*. *If* Caucasian. Meaning coopting trends or fashion statements. From refugees of imperialism. E.g. white matrons in saris. As fake edgy as faux-wildness of British public gardens. R watching us reproachfully. Hating spoiling dinner. Not to mention loathing comparisons. Mustering susceptible physiognomy behind large glasses. Saying despite uniformity of appearance. In Paris—one doing as one feeling. Just not discussing it. The French forever trying to maintain balance. Between order and animal within. R serving up as proof—common expression c'est normal, it's natural. Everything being *nor-mal*. Unless spoiling harmony of surface. He further opining eternal to-point-of-obsessive concern with sensual side of things. Likely safety valve. Permitting continual low-scale release. Of deep unruly passions. Which otherwise. Verging on explosion.

70. Luxembourg. First nice day in ages. I circling basin. Among old French queens. Placed as if on chessboard. Pigeons on heads. In sandbox yet another female statue. Naiad. Or goddess. Children playing under statue's stone breasts. Little navy suits. Soft leather shoes. Red. Yellow. Blue. Rosy cheeks. Smiling up at mother substitute. An edge to air. When clouds slipping over. Then cool and shivery. But not icy blade of autumn. Like chez nous.

Speaking of mothers: now in nice café. Off little triangular square. Near Gertrude Stein's place. Reading most heartbreaking story I yet hearing. In paper. From one of those low-rental highrises. Beyond enclave. On way to Versailles. Thin cardboard walls. Seeping problèmes de voisinage. Article saying euphemistically. I.e. lack of privacy from neighbours. La victime—always au féminin in French—young male teen. Stabbed by buddies. In boy-gang retribution. After victim's mother murdering his father. Boy fleeing taunts of other boys. For weeks. Before turning round. In self-defence. Horror of being hunted. Added to loss of parent. And who killing Cock Robin. Another boy whose mother recently. Abandoning him. And Daddy.

Here—possible racist twist. In trying to convey boy's total terror. Word Muslim getting insinuated behind word retribution. By newspaper. As if causal to narrative. Then by "us" (readers). In quartier voisinant, neighbouring Luxembourg. Where word voisinage, neighbours. Implying—proximity of café tables. And it occurring to me. Avoiding interpretative i.e. cause-and-effect narrative. Likely requiring B's method. Of montage of found objects. Broken toys. Harsh corridors. Discrimination's motivating stench. Juxtaposed on spirited beauty of Raï. Editorial from local Arab weekly. Condemning immigration policy. Cigarettes under towel. Of girl in Hammam. Drawn together by magic of "free" association. Still—I wondering. How much chance connections. Completely free of arbiter.

These close tables encouraging us. To know our neighbour. Man beside. Saying to companion. Lasciviously eyeing my hair.

I think rather they're for profit. She retorting mildly.


71. Today bright and sunny. Celebrating. Walking up Rennes. Translucent water droplets burning into mist. Around architecturally disastrous '70s-style fifty-two-storey glass tour Montparnasse. Left towards gardens. Water burbling down steps of Médicis fountain. Cool pool. With Polyphemus about to crush lovers Acis et Galatea. With rock. Emaciated AIDS man. Crawling from bushes behind. After taking a shit. Lover waiting matter-of-factly. Also with spots on face. Warming in sun.

I too raising physiognomy. Toward flawless blue sky. When who materializing. But T! All in red leather. Tight red curls. Red computer shoulder-bag. Red leather dress. On way to Amsterdam. Or Köln. Career on the rise. But first a little tan. The well-organized highly attractive artist. Making use of every minute. We stopping to look at figure of reclining male. Framed by vines. Himself looking down on ring of pink flowers. Surrounded by perfect ring of grass. For some reason. Both of us laughing.

Walking on. Suddenly complicit. We discussing public gardens. As tropes. *She* acknowledging wild edge of British park. Bordering on hysterical. While *I* conceding French geometric keep-off-grass approach. Suspiciously *fastidious*. Citing Saint Simon's ideal square. Cited in B. Totally made-to-order. Lush with trees in painted cardboard. Flowers in taffeta. They even placing artificial birds in branches. Singing all day long. Thus preserving pleasures of natural environment. Without its muck or clutter. We further agreeing question of gardens more complex. Than simple binaries. French and British both in fact affecting. Certain affinity to nature. British. Miming conqueror. As in "riding to foxes." While French trying to tame. As in Colette's panthers. Or those pigs on a string. Digging up truffles.

We now sitting on wiggly terrasse iron chairs. Drinking espresso. T rolling cigarette. Wonderful crinkly neck. Watching little dog. With painfully short clipped ears. Trotting past our feet. Musing how convenient that contemporaneous Western philosophy. Condemning thinking in opposites. Just as technology transforming night/day. Winter/summer. Past/future. To dots on screen. I.e. time as intermittence. Though body still lagging behind. A little. T laughing. When flying from continent to continent. She adding: trick of feeling good. While keeping on move. Being to perceive "one's" self as part of all those little molecules out there. They're everywhere. These youngish women artists. Got up with the individual style. Of snazzy cartoon figures.

Walking home along winding rue de Grenelle. Night is falling. When noticing in embrasure of building. Little woman sleeping. Flat on back. Neat round little head snug in some kind of bonnet.

Long skirt gathered round her. Neat boots laced up tight to ankles. Like Victorian doll. Rather old. I thinking.

72. R phoning from lovenest. Having been to préfecture. For purpose of securing carte de séjour, work permit. Where he immediately ordered. Into expeditious line. Rapidly outflanking those— mostly from "south"—in non-expeditious queue. Who waiting there for hours. Then R given disconcertingly casual interview. Official expressing interest in his "box." Fashionable square purselike briefcase. He happening to be carrying. Why bother—official declaring. When R asking how to go about. Applying for proper papers. But I was told I need them. R protesting. Oui, logiquement, mais vous êtes canadien; yes in principle, but you are Canadian. Official finally recommending him to préfecture in Caen. Where R giving courses.

   Now I feeling really silly.

73. South on ave de l'Observatoire. Thinking paranoia (fear). Maybe replacing 19th Baudelarian spleen. As principle neurosis. Because of over-efficient contemporaneous policing. Having received one more envelope. With neatly ripped corner. Delivered Tuesday. Plus persistent buzz. On telephone wire. But learning how to distribute fear. On faces in windows. Which windows. Mirroring in passing. Writer heading for luncheon. With leisure lottery administration. White shirt with two rows of stitching round victory collar. Black suit jacket. Appearing in broken sets. In succeeding boutique windows. As in broken $_I{}^I$ of B's narrating spleen. Disrupted by thin lines or spaces. Between montage segments.

   Through door in wall. Massive green lawn. Dining room with huge French windows. Opening on garden with statues. Flirty male on left. Sensual French lips. Suddenly turning cool. On right perfumed female wonder. Using intimate "tu" in private conversation. Walking down hall. Then formal "vous" in company of others. After I *publicly* saying "tu" to her. Covering faux-pas. By suddenly blurting out. To white-gloved waiter. What that on my plate. Never having seen foie gras whole in its little jelly before. Which benightedness further getting projected. On wrinkled physiognomy. Of little dowager opposite. Who claiming she singlehandedly spreading French language. Across anglo provinces in Canada. What a *job* I declaring. Lips twitching mockingly. Then standing. E-elated. More e-elated than intended. Having suddenly remembered. Guests coming to dinner.

Racing through market. Nearly closing. Inclining slightly forward. Buying red lettuce. Blue plums. Pink fish. Black oysters. Buying yellow chicken. I'm a nice leetle cheecken. Saying butcher. As usual trying to flirt. Throwing it in oven. Forty garlic cloves. Colette's recipe. The lovely odour seeping out the door. Penetrating corridors. It smells of gas concierge saying. Knocking. Allegedly pro-German. As we sampling the olives. R and lover beaming serenely. Plus bottle of Château Pouilly. Waiting for P. Waiting. Waiting. She finally showing up. Having fallen asleep on bus. Until les Invalides. *Her* wine bottle rolling up and down aisle. Hair on end. Saying sardonically. You people in faubourg. Think Paris's a white city. And I noticing for first time. Her skin. Café au lait. When the roses sliding from her cheeks. We drink. We drink. We drink.

74. Weather. Icy blue. Then grey. Waiting. Concierge not bringing up mail. Meaning 1. There is none. 2. She not feeling like it. Across street—head on side of steamer trunk. Shining. Green. Orange. Yellow. As if tinted with some fluorescent product. Gazing towards display window on right. Where two exquisite suits flat on stomachs. Square shoulders facing their two bald squished rubber heads of rubbies. Decadently eyeballing each other.

75. Today to London. For purpose of getting new stamp in passport. When re-entering at Dunquerque. Good for three months.

Maybe also see an editor.

Métro. Gare du Nord. Dragging baggage through crowd amassed at doors. Wagon starting up. Suitcase still sticking out. Heading beyond enclave. Into suburbs. On platform outside. Men of Paris huddling. Little groups. From everywhere. On globe. Talking. Making deals. Having followed crowd. From métro stop. To train. Through hole blasted in stone. As if still war. Into old part of station. Under glass-and-iron ceiling. Final espresso. At stand. Outside gate. Old train's frumpy red interior. Empty seats. Heading towards channel. Surfing over fields. Fog. Rain. Reading Proust. Naturellement. His incredible description of gare Saint-Lazare: . . . *Great glass workshop. Where I used to go to catch the train for Balbec, and which spread out over its gap in the city one of those immense skies, of an almost Parisian modernity from Mategna or Verona, under which only the worst most solemn thing could take place, such as a departure, or the raising (erection) of the cross . . .*

77. Back. Dropping bags in studio. Racing to café. Doors now shut against autumnal racket of confluence. At du Bac/Saint-Germain/Raspail. The dock. The saint. The general. Ordering espresso. So glad to be here. After land of stained tea cozies. Dusty chintz. Hedgehogs. Low buildings. Single-family dwellings. With their bit of garden. Too spread-out. Immenseness of London. Taking swift wing of swallow one whole day to cross. Some French poet claiming. Which poet further complaining. London lacking geometric order. Palaces planted. Without regard for symmetry. Or replaced. By massive modern towers. Since devastating war.

Overshadowing tiny ways and alleys. Called Gutter. Milk Street. Iron Monger. Grocer's Lane. Russia Trump. Tropes of ancient London. Paris so unburned. A miracle. Of duplicity—some saying. Or: Paris a woman.

And the publisher in his mews.

Sitting on his fingers.

But. Back. Watching dusk spreading. Behind thick grey clouds. Above roof-garden of grey 19th-century building. Diagonally across. Looking like huge upside-down ship. With oeils-de-boeuf for portholes. Rain. Wind. Huge storm blowing up. On TV people in southeast. Boating from second-storey houses. Of 19th— or earlier—cut stone. In French countryside. Flooded for third time. In as many weeks. Woman pointing to mud. Weeping I just cleaned it up. Sleeves rolled up in French housewife determination. To keep things squeaky clean. No letters. Already waiting for that British publisher to reply. As painful as a love affair. One can wait forever.

The concierge looking worse. Misdelivering mail. Peering through her loupe. I given two addressed to Mademoiselle C D. That gorgeous leather brunette living two floors up. Working for the media. Then Madame X cutting furballs off her ancient crabby Persian. Cutting end off his tail. Quantities of blood. Leaning over it. In blue-patterned Marks & Spencer dress. Sometimes with sweater. French clothes don't fit her. Otherwise *hating* the English. And women. Je les HAÏS. Je haïs TOUTES LES FEMMES, I hate all women. She roaring. At previous studio occupant. When told who coming next.

I hear her ex collaborated.


78. In Saint-Germain. Again. Against wall. Handsome French schoolgirls. Well-brushed locks. Falling over eye. Pink lips. Crossed chunky heels. Watching world ironically. E.g. working-class Brits. Now coming through door. Nondescript jeans. Oil-dipped jerseys for keeping out rain. Bored. Drinking beer. In Paris. Wondering what to do. Leg shaking under table. Looking up expectantly at

tulip lampshades. Down crimson walls. Kind of pretty. One saying hopefully. Wistful tone touching protective or guilty chord chez moi. Rendering his failure to glance repeatedly. At moi chéri. In ubiquitous café mirrors. Sign of innocence. Unlike French males. Tossing back heads. Fingers through curls. As preened as *Golden Eyes*'s Tom. Spending two hours grooming feet alone. While declaring to friend from Provence: *Women love fops!* Fabulous self-care apparently suggesting huge potential. For caring for other.

I adding layer of lipstick. Guilty note still pulsing. Mother being Protestant. B saying remorse unequivocally *19th*. It being sole emotion that century. Feeling with sincerity. As in those sons of leisured classes. Whose grey cloaks lined with scarlet. I.e. effeminate. Allegedly flagging regret. For crimes of papa. While we. Sitting on divans. Turning off Sarajevo. Rwanda. Bosnia. Not to mention documentary from chez nous. Re: uranium. In reservation rivers.

*Not* wishing to go to fundraiser. Either. Against war weapon RAPE. In ex-Yugoslavia. Rehearsing some excuses. For S. Too late to venture. Onto strange métro lines. In distant neighbourhoods. Someplace called Picpus. Trying this one on P. On phone. She bursting out laughing.

79. *"Dispersion"*

Instead of fundraiser. Meeting C. For protest exhibition of young artists. In abandoned mills and warehouses. About to be demolished. Near quai de la Gare. Except she not there. Not at bottom of inside métro stairs. Leading down to station exit. Not at foot of crooked crazy outside steps. Leading up to high blue railway bridge. Several cops. Checking Africans stepping off trains. Therefore I crossing to café opposite. Pretending to phone. Notwithstanding new stamp in passport saying DUNQUERQUE, 05 OCT. Implying I freshly arrived tourist. Then C materializing. Cigarette in air. Smooth bowl haircut. Those admirable full lips.

We strolling along quay. Industrial Seine lapping at feet. Past giant chantier, construction site. Of new Bibliothèque nationale.

Futuristic restatement. Of Second Empire athanaeum. On right bank. As well as monument. To left-leaning president. Who once collaborating. Due to "lacking information." Construction. Devouring ancient warehouse quarter. Young (poor) artists' last urban refuge. Like everywhere. I thinking. Climbing dusty winding stairs. Mansard roofs on turrets. Great air of poverty. Youth with baseball caps à l'américain. I.e. backwards. Advancing mid sanguine air of making do. Crumbling plaster walls. Sound-tracks. Mobiles. Comics. Theme apparently: *Dispersion*. My favourite: scroll-mural of cartoon-like middle-aged creators. From *Renaissance* to *Surrealism*. While young artists "realistically"—slipping off scroll bottom. Old video terminal in middle. Scoping *us*. Departing. C being québécoise. I.e. positively republican. Disliking scroll's representing negatively our abjection. Preferring abstraction. Of copper polished swords. In courtyard below. Leaning together. In heavily glinting sun. Out for a minute. Or forest of bamboos. Wound with blood-coloured cloth. My eye dwelling on bright blue railway bridge. Yonder.

Returning along quay. Feeling cheated. Having seen nothing elating. Crossing pont de la Tournelle. Under ugly geometric Sainte Geneviève: Patroness of Paris. Nice pair of porkchops in bag. To prepare with old French recipe. Mustard and cream. Over pont Marie. Feeling morally superior. The way tourists do when beholding faults in their host. Getting back at "them." For looking down on "us." C citing some '80s French biennial. Where no women painters. Her query to curator earning rejoinder. Remarquez il n'y a pas de boîteux non plus, there are no cripples either. Opening the wine—I venturing opinion French current avant-garde maybe in suburbs. Ruby glass glinting exquisitely. We drink.

Walking home along Saint-Germain. Still vaguely guilty. About ex-Yugoslavia benefit. Looking up. Seeing I in middle of mime performance. Mime staring at me. Very lost and frightened. Surrounding crowd laughing. I stepping behind kiosque. And peering out at him. Trying to be cool.

80. Clouds. Cold. Getting up. Shaking off disillusionment. About not seeing any good painting. French being over-interested in technique. Which thoughts collapsing in silly heap. Adding to day of dégâts matéraiux, material disasters. Huge German television falling off console. While vacuuming. Crashing to floor. Denting hardwood. Also in falling—taking chunk from gleaming varnished contour. Of art-deco armchair. After which computer screen image crooked. Frame leaning sideways. Print on a bias. Walking later. In brightening sun. Hoping inner sense of disaster. Dissolving in minute. Hoping that only a *small* black cloud. Floating over head.

Now on Edgar-Quinet. Having forgotten blue pen at home. Spoiling blue surface of graph book. Continuing with black. Brought by waiter on tray. Never wanting to leave. This place. Its sanguine discipline. Surrounding outer "one." Gertrude Stein saying. With civilized atmosphere. While leaving inner space. For being own person. True—sense of inner decay since London. Watching sun glinting off dyed hair of women. Mostly to cover grey. Women of certain age. (Me soon!) I wondering how to make beautiful. Yet admitting decay under. What lacks/biases. It helpful to admit. What hindering. Lucky Baudelaire. Belonging to century where nihilism still worn on physiognomy. As emblem of progress. Negativity not having been appropriated. By apparati of domination. Though painter Courbet saying Baud's face changing. Often as a mime's.

And I turning face. Gently. Towards sun. Noticing tenderness of men. On whose shoulders women leaning. Stroke of a hand. Softness of a glance. Astonishing. Because unexpected. This tenderness. On Sunday.


80 *bis*. Tonight civil war in Moscow. Watching on TV. The White House where Communists holed up. In Red Square sympathizers gathering. Some of army shooting. Some not. Divided. At least in Moscow. From White House balcony Communist after Communist. Calling for the whole army to rally. For The People to occupy

the television stations. Language similar. At least in structure of rhetoric. To accounts of 1917 Revolution. Each speaker imagining he Lenin.

It is this past rotting in the centre. Saying they won't win.

81. Yesterday walk with S. In Hôtel du Nord neighbourhood. Of film-noir fame. What a treat walking with her! City coming alive in entirely different ways. Crossing place de la République. Arm gesturing right toward brown potted goose. From her region. Piled in window. Left towards little boutique hawking reminiscences. From several revolutions. Down at crypt holding dissidents. From 1830 and 1848. Past a grisette, working woman's statue. For this a people's quarter. Apron gathered up. Little face looking down at canal Saint-Martin. Endless mirror. Refracting brown sky.

We ambling along leafy banks. Locks. Curved bridges. Birds in brown air. With what's happening in Russia—I piping up—we'll soon all be nostalgic for the Soviets! Past old factories. Renovated condominiums. Past Hôtel du Nord. *Closed.* Her peaked cap. Rejecting word nostalgia. Saying *au contraire*. Events in east ultra-important for contemporaneity. Because ultimately affecting. Western way of seeing. Were she an artist. She starting there. Canal bowing right. But what does she mean. Does she mean illuminating spark released. When new Russian gangster-style raw capitalist individualism. And withered so-called classless society clashing. Canal bowing left. Or maybe she referring to traces still remaining. From brief apogée, utopia. Of Soviets. Early post-Revolution. Worker—being militant—learning history. Artist—political—being versed in social theory. Politician—reading poetry. Malheureusement ending with prison bars. Of gulag. Passing checked woman. Feeding brown and white pigeons. By La Villette basin. Such a huge mirror. Over which endless barges. Formerly rushing meat slaughtered on banks. To Paris. Now banks of high-rises. With gulls like in Vancouver. Dwarfed in the gleam.

But a writer can only write. What she knowing.

Along canal de l'Ourcq. In whose brown surface a crystal science dome reflected. Once mirroring rippling face of Baudelaire. Was canal water then bloody. Did air yet reek of stench. Where sun gilding *alike the city and the fields / parching the stubble / and sinking into slums.* We stepping under la périphérique, Paris circumference route. Way blocked by cranes. Hills of gravel. Suburbs beyond. Atop high embankment just under girders. Bright ragpile. Pot. One shoe. Someone's abode. Leading me to mention young squatters' exhibition. C and I finding lacking. In innovation.

S "dialectical": But it was crawling with people.

Brown dusk falling. Retracing steps southward. S trotting quicker. Past La Villette basin. Canal Saint-Martin. Across Seine to student quarter. Left foot blistering. Right to S's street in Montparnasse. Brown dusk now turned to black. Carrying roast chicken in brown paper bag. Past '70s-type cinema. Old sofas. Cement floor. People reading periodicals. Past iron curtains of already-closed shops. Still-beckoning pastry windows. White apartment in inner courtyard. Art-deco fretwork on window. Putting on disc of Russian women songs. From camps in Siberia. *"Don't Wait for Me Papa."* Eating the roast chicken. With shiny red peppers. Her dark deep-set almost Spanish eyes.

82. B saying in detective novel. Hero feeling suspect himself. Hence projecting suspicion (paranoia) on someone in crowd. Later in film-noir. This blurring of edges. Between subject and object. Of narrative. Represented by tinctured treatment of filmstrip. Displaced onto women characters. Creating dangerous fascinating heroines. Wearing "suspect." Like emblem. Except inner voice saying: already forty-two. I thinking *I wish*. Sky growing greyer. Remembering needing camera fixed. Requiring trip. To faubourg Saint-Antoine. Rare "authentic" Parisian quarter. Remaining. Behind Père Lachaise cemetery. Inhabitants still saying—going *down* to Paris. Modest boulevards. Ancient printing presses. Where once seeing doll-like junkie girl on corner. One seeing in all the major cities. Scratching her stocking. More parsing clouds. Dozing off

to sleep. Ambiguous (suspect) dream. Of feeling contained. By several African children! In hotel courtyard. Perfect inversion of article. Read earlier in *Libé*. Famous Zaïrois rumba singer. Refused asylum though wife dead mysteriously. Daughter fourteen raped. Back in Zaïre. The French esteeming family having no good reason. For needing refuge. His handsome lined face in photo. Against ad for French coats with fur collars. Forties-style mannequins. Fleshy faces. Hair high. Artist-model joints. Picture cutline: *Without papers you're finished*. Waking. I turning to *Doll Konvolut*, section. In B. Opening with citation. From 19th-century German woman writer.

*I am the sole doll's breast with feelings.*

83. In Russia army shooting Communists. In window across street—suit jackets earlier leaning forward. Chins on the ground. Round rubber foreheads touching. Aggressive. Now leaning away from each other. So backs flat on floor. In gesture of abjection or vulnerability. Thus displaying bright wide ties and shirts. Between lapels. Of jackets. Behind them on wall. Row of portraits. Dark. Heavy frames. Can't see what they are. Maybe dogs.

Speaking of dogs. In eras of conservatism. Interesting how "one." Emphasizing vulgarities. To fit expectations of Other. E.g. yesterday calling leisure studio owner. Saying l'évier *bloqué*. Franglais for l'évier *bouché*, sink's blocked. He majesterially ironic.—You wanting me to come round and scratch it. Later P explaining. In Paris drains lifted out and scraped. Trying this in kitchen. Drain separating entirely. From drainpipe in hands. Great rush of water. Flooding down behind cupboard. The better to drip on concierge's leather sofa. Just underneath in foyer. Where she sitting. Radio to ear.

Quickly crossing lobby. Calling bonjour Madame. Au revoir Madame. Simultaneously trying to glance at ceiling over sofa. For telltale watermarks. Outside cold and windy. Métro to Porte-Dauphine in 16$^e$. Now frankly raining beyond art-nouveau glass petals over exit portal. Over art-nouveau balconies along 16$^e$'s sumptuous avenue Foch. On one of which balconies Deneuve's *Belle de Jour,* classy callgirl. Standing. Ca '65. In tailored skirt. Pumps. Smiling vaguely. Having nearly got husband bumped off.

Turning left on rue Pergolèse. Pelvis forward. Geometric hair. Flapping in breeze. Into brightly renovated salon. Electric blue geometric-shaped sofas. Chrome. Stark white walls. Authors from chez nous. Biker jackets. T-shirts. Torn jeans. À la mode in Americas. Je me suis fait attaquer, I got mugged—one writer cracking. Mock-embarrassed. Pointing to knee. Sticking out of pantleg. Quatuor suddenly breaking into a cappella concert. Voices stretched to flute. Piano. Percussion. Associations sonorous. Reminiscent of '40s *automatisme*—as we calling surrealism chez nous. Poet Gauvreau's *Jappements,* barkings . . . *Achia chichenéchiné chachouann gduppt.* Jeaned knees. Tapping out beat. Feet pounding. One in baseball cap. Some little plastic thing twirling round on top. To nodding of head.

Behind—C arguing. With French film critic. Little Tintin cowlick. Hushed phonemes re: Godard's latest production. *Hélas pour moi.* God coming to earth. To live in guy's buttock-grabbing body. For purpose of exploring romantic love's mysteries. With someone's faithful unsuspecting wife. Ça ne vaut rien, useless. Misogynous. C's husky voice intoning. The critic beside himself. Saying C not "moderne." Taking tropes. For reality. We walking out. Still raining in 16$^c$. Under glass canopy of métro she blurting. Homos worse than hétéros these days. Meaning critic. I saying nothing. Wanting to stay afloat. To stay out of categories. Moving back and forth. Across comma of difference. A gerund. Or gesture.


84. Concierge knocking on door. Saying all the rain giving her bronchitis. And nightmares. Last night dreaming her husband coming and taking inside of her TV. I supposing that like taking her heart. Her eyes puffier and puffier. Wearing two sweaters. Over Marks and Spencer dress. Head turning this way and that. Trying to look. Over shoulder. At huge TV on black studio console. Re-playing

programme called *Divan*. With philosopher. Sitting feet up on yellow leather chaise longue. Shouting image usurping space. In "communications explosion." Formerly reserved. For critical writing/thinking. While speaking he manifestly growing angrier and angrier. Gesticulating unbuttoned right cuff. On which eye of viewer necessarily focussing. I turning down sound. Wondering if cuff unbuttoned on purpose. Making philosopher more interesting. Because simultaneously negating and substantiating own discourse. For being unbuttoned. Meaning something. In appearance-conscious Paris.

    Eczema getting worse.

85. Window changed again. A suit standing up. Very fine check. Huge wide brightly striped scarf. Wrapped around torso. As tightly as mummy. So arms can't move. Seeming oddly obverse reflection. Of last night's cinema documentary. *Femmes de Galère, Pigeonholed Women*. About Paris's "best" female prison. On outskirts. Three thousand inmates. Mostly prostitutes. Majority addicts. 45 per cent HIV-positive. Some having babies. Touching camera work. Following women "out." Trying to make a life. See you later. Guard cracking to blonde. In back of departing van. Naturellement no one will hire them. Bad hotels. Tiny saggy rooms with kitchen counter folding up wall. Making room for bed. Unable to afford even socks for baby. Naturellement forced back into street. The first fix. Such a relief. Only one woman. Young and pretty. "Saved." By liberal film director. Giving her work. She laying head gratefully on his shoulder. Audience. Fine-smelling intellectuals. Clucking approvingly.

    Going back to studio. Métro Rambuteau platform. Which seeming eerily empty earlier. Once again crowded. As befitting heart-of-Paris station. Men again asleep on benches. Having hidden shoes under sleeping bodies. So nobody stealing. Grabbing forty winks. Before getting kicked off. Out at Saint-Sulpice. Down narrow rue de Grenelle. Smell of fish drawing attention to little recess of building. Where neat Victorian-style woman in long skirt and bonnet. Sleeping before. Big guy red and muscular. Now opening can of tuna. Equipped with can opener. Sleeping bag. Heater. Did he kick her out. The inhabitants of great cities. Trod on daily. Some poet saying.

Flicking on TV. Huge rafale, police raid at Rambuteau. Just before I disembarking there for film. This explaining why métro empty. On arriving. Three hundred and fifty checked for papers. Sixteen arrested. Though I likely safe with DUNQUERQUE entry stamp. Unless nervous tic of physiognomy. Giving away. The trick being when dealing with cops. Or any authority. Hiding all capacity for disobedience. By keeping eyes empty.

86. On TV rain coming down. Slant. Now people in south*west*. Getting flooded out. More tearful women. Having dug belongings from mud and sludge. Time and time again. Concentrated scrubbing. Will Seine be next. Exhaling its effluence. Like its breath. Through streets. The air of Paris. A republican notion. A synthesis.

Floods in England too.

But mother of P's Polish friend. Saying suburbs *full* of magpies. Meaning—weather about to improve. Speaking of flooding. Making terrible mess in studio. Rushing to get ready for literary festival. When kettle boiling dry. Lifting lid. From its citation art-deco triangular form. Great white chunks of kettle's bottom. Rattling inside. Looking closer. Seeing they only thick chalk-like coating of residue. Of Paris water. Breaking loose. Rushing to take shower. Nozzle popping out of holder. And flooding bathroom with steamy deluge. Running through lobby. Looking up again over shoulder. To see if all this water I insisting on leaking. Seeping through plaster. Above concierge's leather sofa.

Instead of turning right. Towards Champs-Élysées theatre. Where Paris's best actors. Polishing already over-polished sentences. From Francophonie's margins. Before descending into theatre basement restaurant. For croquettes and juicy baked tomatoes. Mirroring suppers. In colonies. I crossing Luxembourg. And exiting near Panthéon. Where at certain times of day. Shadow of hotel begetting surrealism. Creeping across square. Hoping maybe a little André Breton in air. Who himself. Constantly creating shock or surprise. By setting alarm. For going off. Before sentence ending. But in café. Only woman honeymooner. Blonde rosy-cheeked '60s-American-in-Paris-movie look. Ordering porkhocks. Remembering junior year abroad. Also moonfaced student from chez nous. Talking obsessively to French girl about identity. Without Québec independence—c'est la catastrophe.

Anyway. Writing this. Just below Panthéon. When looking up and what to my astonishment—young woman going by on bike. Looking exactly like Z! Golden brown curls. Riding directly towards monument. Under which France's great men buried. With dome and fluted columns. Holding up pediment. AUX GRANDS HOMMES LA PATRIE RECONNAISSANTE. Writ large across top. To left—law faculty. LIBERTÉ. ÉGALITÉ. FRATERNITÉ—dictum of French Revolution. Printed on façade. Cyclist veering right toward Hôtel des Grands Hommes. Where first automatic writing experiments allegedly taking place. Geraniums in windows. I walking towards it. Girl has disappeared. Looking to left. Only half-visible pretty renaissance façade of Saint-Étienne-du-Mont. Called florid by Henry James.

Home through Luxembourg. Past guy selling chestnuts. By gate. Past Marie de Médicis's pool. Cop behind bench. Preparing to ask sleeping African for papers. Yellow autumn foliage. Looking up—I noticing Panthéon on left's in perfect line with tour Eiffel. On right—two arrondissements away. Looking north—it forming a perfect line with Notre-Dame. Standing there. In middle of cross. Feeling momentarily resentful. Of centuries-old goal. Of making Paris object of luxury.

87 "Walk with S" *bis*.

Damp and foggy. Smell of geraniums and moisture. Through slightly opened windows. Of CAFÉ SAINT-GERMAIN. Feeling S and I will argue. The last time I in Rome. Smooth French voice saying. Articulating like angel. Like Proust. Every syllable groomed to perfection. I wanted to go by foot, c'était la catastrophe. Then lowering to caress. Raving about Carravaggio's Saint Jean Baptiste painting.

C'était la splendeur.

Waiting. I taking deep contented sniff. Of splendid café ambience. Drinking carafon of rouge. Brought by small dark woman-hating waiter. S right behind. Holding precious card. For entering famous Second Empire reading room of old BIBLIOTHÈQUE NATIONALE. Whose famous glass dome. Floating high above desks. Designed in 19th technological way. For permitting longest extension possible. Of *natural* light. Of day. Pinned serendipitously. By means of slender iron columns. Here and there to earth. Under which—users' breaths. Plus breeze of countless turning pages. Disturbing dust on leaves of room's high lush foliage-painted panels. B sentimentalizing. It being under this panoply. He dreaming up Paris arcades book.

Crossing pont du Carrousel. Passing Molière's statue. Passing wine-store window. With Dufy watercolour of perfect young men. Plus army recruiters. Sign saying: *Sveltest youth coming from wine-growing regions.* Reading room malheureusement so crowded. With annual book-fair visitors. Seeing nothing but countless little lamps on tables. Installed post-electricity. Before being propelled out other door. Into GALÉRIE COLBERT. Where book-fair stands set up. S stopping to talk to well-preserved woman. Air of militant from '70s. Who declaring in astonishment—she a grand-mother. It happening just like that. Very unexpected. Woman repeating several times. Waiting I rifling through displays. In search of contemporaneous literary avant-garde. Not knowing where to look. No patience to persist. Nice stand run by old couple. Selling small paperback editions. Of classics once considered dangerous. E.g. rare or little-known tales. By Dostoevsky.

1993. *Not* a grand cru.

Then Palais-Royal café. S's deep-set eyes opposite. Crushed right up against couple eating fried eggs. Trop cuits saying pink and blonde wife. Pleasantly enough. Husband very sour. Wincing visibly when our shoulders brushing. Maybe this why S and I suddenly loudly discussing. Huge gay demonstration in Washington. After Clinton election. I decrying predominance of banners. Demanding gay rights *in military*. S serving up lesson in materialist dialectics. Fingers touching as if playing cat's cradle. On one hand it necessary to consider who regularly enlisting: working-class kids—notably African-American. Wanting democratic rights . . . I—*Yes*. But. Shouldn't we be aiming away from militaristic solutions. Using slogans more convulsive. DON'T FIGHT—*FIST!* I suggesting pruriently. She implying I distanced from reality.

Pink-lipped woman watching. Bemused. Husband cloaked in sullenness. Maybe old militants. May '68. To left well-chiselled youth. Confident of beauty. Hustling girl in tight striped shirt. Seventies back in fashion. His eyes mesmerized. The way papa taught him. S saying some gays signing up to find their kind. Some wishing to virilize. Or oppositely. To convert war machine to peace corps. I saying she too non-critical of patriotism. Voice rising emotionally. Betraying secret envy. Of self-assertive citizen. Fostered in well-militarized republics.

88. In display window opposite. Expensive scarf no longer wrapped mummy-like. Around suit's torso. Instead hands of suit are pulling fine Persian rug. Out from under feet of another suit. Who has fallen on his prat. Shiny boots waving in air. Gesture ambivalent. More like sexual play. Than violence. Heading for right bank again. Past Molière. Smudged poster of Situationist founder Debord. RIONS DE NOTRE INCONSCIENT. Into little square opposite old Bibliothèque nationale. Right on Richelieu. To square Louvois. Bibliothèque's green antechamber. To look at those four delicious buxom women. Glimpsed yesterday with S. On fountain in middle. Representing important French rivers. La Seine. La Sôane. La Loire. La Garonne. The curves of their forearms. "Softness" of breasts. Right on Chabanais. Eczema unbearable. Past world-famous brothel. Closed in '47. Entering bar

H-the-anarchist earlier refusing to enter. Tables with gorgeous peonies on them. Older women with poodles. And ingénues. Beside them. Tailored outfits with starched open collars. Drinks too expensive. Ordering coffee at counter. Two younger women in corner. Giving *French Kiss* deepest meaning possible. American appearing. In driving gloves and jodhpurs. Also ordering "just coffee for now." Large blonde sailor-type smoking. Watching her charges. From her place behind cash.

Raining in Sarajevo.

89. The sun which would help eczema. Only appearing on sudden bed of ruffled blue. At dusk. Right bank once more. To photograph Cirque d'Hiver, Winter Circus. Circular pink building. With scarlet frieze of prancing horses. By little park. Near Bastille. Site for possible anecdote. At end of Bk of MW. I considering calling. *To the Winter Circus.* Mirroring *To the Finland Station.* At beginning of century. End-of-century mirror. Naturellement inverted. E.g. scenes on TV. Hinting at massacre of Communists. Holed up in "White House." By Yeltsin's troops. Everybody contemporaneously scurrying to prove loyalty to post-Commie President. No trace of lost and wounded. "Conservative" the press calling the Reds. Yeltsin then "revolutionary!" Then spying poster. On Cirque's painted wall. Stepping closer. It turning out to be poster of Leatherman. Announcing (in English) huge GAY PARTY. *Yesterday!*

Now in ancient tea room in Jewish/gay quarter. Outside people rushing down Vieille-du-Temple. Where Knights Templar Order reigning. Until massacred. Ca 1300. Some saying for sodomy. Or king wanting their property. Tea-room patron. Hair black and slicked back. Sweeping tiled floor. While I trying to imagine narrator. Neither too distanced. Nor spleenish. This maybe requiring frequent changing. Of position or angle. Like those intersecting eyes/V's. Alternately upright/inverted. Of tile pattern. On Coupole floor. Or maybe structuring movement of narration. As in various tile-floor arrangements. Depending on class/quartier of café-tabac. In question. *Harsh* black-and-white for AIDS drop-in bar. Near Bastille. *Miniature* beige ceramic squares covered with butts. In working people's cafés. *Fake* brick for provincial tourist-attracting places. Or here—*pockmarked* blue-and-white. Very ancient. Renewed with dark blue strips of newer marble. Latter seeming to hold former together.

Ordering tarte Tatin. I saying accidentally tante Tatin. The lush tarte edges like those buxom aunts. One loves to hug. Soft breasts spilling over stays. Gooey delicious apple-y cake. Spilling over pan edges. On shiny copper counter. Beside it a giant coupe of plastic fruit. Fairly real-looking "fruit." Tinged mirrors. Also coffee. Outside more people rushing. Past windows with Stars of David painted on them.

Soon time to go. At bus stop—elderly woman. Very lovely skin. Despite slightly red nose. As if liking to take a drink. Saying how her legs hurt. Me smiling sympathetically. She instantly remarking on quality of my teeth. Adding hers once nice. Smiling. So I can see they're worn to little stumps. Do you have any cavities. Loads I say. Complicitly. At your age! she quipping. Possibly ironic.

But first more coffee. Thinking of the Russians. How in Moscow chauffeurs relieved of BMWs. By armed gangsters. In full glare of sun.


90. Grey. November. Ex-prisonnier ringing bell downstairs. Wanting to repair small articles. Touching slightly twisted physiognomy. Albeit failing to brush past concierge. Slamming heavy door practically on his fingers. Her profile then pivoting almost elegantly on shiny black heel. Pulled up to full height. Bowing courtly from waist. In gesture possibly reminiscent of Vichy. Handing me letter. Small complicit smile. Oh you *too*. Have friends in Germany.


91. Last night with T to see splendid Isabelle Huppert. Playing Woolf's *Orlando*. Under great American director Wilson. Fog falling slightly. Unfortunately small notice on column of Odéon's

half-boarded-up-for-renovations neo-classical façade. Saying *Complet*, Sold Out. But wanting it so badly—*knowing* I'll get in. T applying usual acumen. Standing tall. Russet-headed. Mid court-yard columns. As if somewhere in antiquity. With 100 milling ticketless Parisians. Her conspicuously black-gloved hand holding little sign. So tiny. Man needing to approach to read it. He does. Speaking confidentially in her ear. Jacket over shoulders. Quietly offering his. Acquired from union. At discount.

The gloves did it she whispering gleefully. Racing down hall. As curtain rising under surrealist Masson's ceiling. Yellow swirling. Dress. Boots. Hats. Gesturing towards dark cameos round edges. I feeling envious. Of T's efficiency in self-presentation. Divine Huppert already tiptoeing across stage. Pale. Dressed in knickers: naughty British boy. Uttering—not Virginia's little prince's words. But high spoiled squeals. With fake British accent. Cavorting in profile. Turn-ing magnificent red head. Across curvilinear-lit set. In geometric movements. Yes. Wilson at autistic best. Rendering Woolf's volumi-nous text so divinely abstract. That we. Like young Proust who like-wise going to great boyish lengths to see La Berma (Sarah Bernhardt). Play Phaedra. Not anticipating imminent disappointment.

For suddenly Huppert uttering volley of words. Whole over-crowded sentences. Paragraphs. Pages. Talking. Talking. Irritat-ingly rapid. Covering centuries. In near hysterical chatter. Behind which one seeing not the young prince turning slowly. Into a woman. But nervous voice of spoiled mad Virginia. Miraculously the diva not collapsing from effort. Her divine head and white limbs leaping. Dancing. Overmoving. Soundscape overcharged. To point of imploding. Making one wonder why critics dithyrambic. All pleasure now having ceased. Like young Marcel—no amount of effort. Of straining ears eyes and mind towards stage. Provid-ing anticipated effect. Though perhaps vague impulse of admira-tion provoked by frenzy. Of audience applause.

So that's what Wilson thinks of *us*. I scoffing to T. As we leaving.

*Us?????* She responding testily.

Proust's father also resenting the brash boy's criticism of La Berma's *Phaedra*. Given the esteem in which his dinner guest—the diplomat M. de Norpois—held the diva.

In turn Proust resenting father's saying he Marcel was subject. To time's laws.

Less than two months left. In studio.

92. Sitting in parc Monceau. Watching sun setting obliquely through Arc de Triomphe. Gilding parc's fake ruins. Where youngish Marcel liking to stroll. Who someone calling Persian prince in concierge's loge, cage. Refreshing himself after late-night salons. Down sinewy paths. Once tracing some duke's dream of embracing all time. Within parc's parameters. Which paths originally plunging into exotic hothouse forest. Or into intricate Chinese pagoda with mirrors painted as arabesques. One—a surprise-mirror—opening into garden in underground gallery. Wall panels painted with trompe l'oeil images. Then— barely pre-Revolution—parc muted. In keeping with rising progressive forces. To "natural" English style. Tinkly nordic streams. Spilling down hillocks. Though still mossy pyramid. Plus Naumachia oval basin. Half-sheltered by frittering Corinthian colonnade. Miming Roman pools constructed for simulating naval battles.

First parachutist also landing there ca 1800.

I getting up and strolling. Midst shiny giant prams. Wheels like coaches. Still pushed by nannies in uniform. As in Marcel's time. Trailing little girls in longish tailored coats. Exquisite dresses in gap of flaps. Along paths arc-ing into shadows of ornate balconies. Paris's finest real estate. Where Marcel—perhaps after tea with Charlus—once leaning. Watching boys on rollerblades. Racing past statue of Musset. Chopin at piano. Muse in swoon at feet. Female angel distributing flowers over. Whilst careful gardeners raking. Grooming. Sweeping sidewalk gutters. In sandbox one contemporaneous-style au pair. Short blonde hair and single earring. Possibly one of "us."

Strolling out gate. Algerian crescent flying. Over embassy. Making me think of hammams. Nice spot for girls. If from more traditional families. Hiding cigarettes under knotted towels. Except cops now posted. Near Arab institutions. Asking for papers. Crossing little square. To quite traditional restaurant/tabac. Marble inlaid bar. Three businessmen. One French. One American. One Puerto Rican. Plotting to build hydro dam. In some ecologically delicate Latin American location. Puerto Rican playing local expert. American image-maker. Saying ecologists anti-dam. Therefore must be perceived as beneficial. For reforestation purposes. Puerto Rican laughing. To get the electricity he saying. First you need the war. Then you need the treaty. Lighting cigarette. Frenchman listening. American ordering more mineral water.

93. In ancient Marais passage des Singes, Monkey Passage. *Not* one of those glass-roofed arcades. B speaking of. But only little alley. Having decided to take time "in stride." Only writing. When wanting to. When suddenly spying T. Entirely in red. Waving like beacon. From narrow sidewalk opposite.

We continuing. Discussing Freud. In snatches. Between popping into little galleries. Featuring new women artists. From elsewhere. Notable chair installation. With curly triangle. Of brown pubic hair on seat. T saying Freud's genius. Breaking neurosis into anecdotal fragments. Which bits and pieces. He then re-constructing. Into master narratives. I saying.—Passing open Sunday window. Two young women inside. Coiffed and made up. Sitting on beds. Babies sleeping soundly.—Maybe we still nostalgic for master explanations. Because wanting to be comforted (or punished). T agreeing torn. Between perpetual need for reassuring storytelling Daddy. And unreassuring lack of solution. Suggested by increasing impulse. Towards thinking in patterns. Which dichotomy ruining generation after generation. In 20th. I inviting her to discuss more over coffee. Definitely attracted. But her afternoon blocked out. Waving redfaced watch—she entering courtyard. Covered with brightly coloured everchanging physiognomies of American Cindy Sherman. Posturing as bawd. Punk. Elizabethan. Grecian.

Or is it now I seeing those young women through the open window. Chatting by sleeping babies. Hurrying on. A little early. To home of French editor. Whose answer still I awaiting. Re: possible French publication of my little Bk of MW. He serving Chinese tea. Brewed to perfection. Delicately. In lovely China cups. His male partner. Plus attractive French lesbian. Nice bangs. Watching from sidelines. Large cat on bed behind. Lighting cigarette. Saying the work fabulous. Très beau. Speaking in ways no one speaking in before. He naturellement wanting to publish. Le hic, catch being. American in charge of translation. Thinking narrative wanting. We joking she fucking the boss. I leave. Empty sign. Walking through rain. Disguised in short blue raincoat. Haircut. In bistro window—seeing statuesque woman. With silver pageboy. Once encountered. Stepping from row of lindens. On les Invalides. Waving gaily. Invitingly. I waving back. "Gail-y." Too.

94. Floating. Whimsical with fatigue. Down pale autumn street. A few hanging leaves. Having spent nuit blanche in Paris! Having taken first métro home. 5:30a. Having waited. In empty place de la Concorde station. For ticket gate to open. When an army of people. Bearing down on me. Running for their lives. The cleaning staff of Paris. Uniformly from "the south." In panic of being fired. Causing immediate deportation. Behind me on platform. Tall handsome African. Red sleepless eyes. Half-hidden in tunnel entrance. In case I a cop. Across tracks another man. Rumpled jeans. Curly-toed runners. Sleeping on bench. I thinking oh he's got away with spending the night. When *hop!* Train passing in other direction. Bench then empty. Between stops exhausted métro riders. Also snatching few seconds' sleep.

Floating. Back to grey-yellow studio. Whimsical. I.e. wishing *things* were different. Having watched elections. On satellite TV at embassy. Young anglo suits on folding chairs in front. Grimly drinking Scotch. Longhaired québécois in leather. At back. Cheering as indépendantiste party moving closer. To national opposition. Rosy western anglo NDP-leaning family seated on floor. Veering right to anti-immigration party. As québécois secessionist votes increasing. Assembly gathered there—uncanny mirror. Of television screen. Young woman from Ottawa. Carefully got up. Careful haircut. Carefully matched lipstick and scarf (badly tied). Cleaning ashtrays. Saying I'll do anything. Not to go back *there*.

T and I. Floating. Onto still dark Champs-Élysées. Past buildings with exquisitely lit fronts. Likely including former habitat of Swann and Odette. In blue-windowed ante-room of which young Marcel waiting for Gilberte. Full of winter orchids. Fire burning in white marble cuve. Valets. Rushing in. Adding water to the former. Coal to the latter. Marcel initially overwhelmed with luxury. Then feeling ressentiment. Gilberte not more attentive. Past TV crew. Waiting outside Champs-Élysées métro. Past park. Past brightly coloured fountain. Past—possibly—two hookers. At end of shift. Past a cop. T—heading east. Toward pont Marie. Likely home to work.

I to faubourg. Falling asleep. Briefly.


95. Now a woman or a man. Woman I think. Glancing my way occasionally from second floor across street. Where she sitting every few days. Two-sided mirror. Reflecting light into my studio. Plucking unwanted hair. On seeing I watching—she aiming beam directly. Into my eyes.

Currently attending small film festival. Where "unwanted hair" not necessarily scorned. Exiting métro near small place de la Contrescarpe. Small grass circle. Drunks. Waiting for Godot. Three small trees. Each so far from other. Seeming completely alone. Up narrow ancient market street. Furry animals hanging. In kiosques. Mosque. Corner boys harassing hooker. Having stolen her purse. She leaning forward. To grab it. Bleached blonde hair. Weathered décolletée. Waist held in by skirtband. Brat tossing it to other. Left on drab street. Rebuilt in '70s. Low ugly stucco community centre.

Decked for occasion with posters of femmes-cuir, leatherwomen. Kissing.

Sight rare in Paris.

Inside dykes running around greeting each other. *Hallo ma poule!* One shouting to another. Across room. Everyone in state of excitement. As if isolation "normal." For older generation. Eating ham. Pasta. Salad. Drinking blanc. Brushcuts. Cigarettes. Tall Dutch girls in boyish tweeds. Large shoes. Much in demand. Greying older women. Sporting facial hair. With aplomb. Younger creamy lipstick dykes. In skirts. Coded by boldness of haircut. Or stance. Not affording me a glance. My haircut artfully hiding forehead. Burning with eczema. Retreating to nearby café. Usual cheap beige tile floor. Blonde hooker—now purseless. On stool. Chatting up guy. Comme si de rien n'était, as if nothing happening earlier. Unfortunately no little square of cheering chocolate. Served on saucer. By thin glass cup.

The films: from East Germany documentary on daily difficulties of being dyke. Under "socialism." From America post-punk queer fashion. Featuring outrageousness. From chez nous sentimental clip. Featuring music and nature. Russians fabulous. Lack of Western-style feminism. Or possibly lack of commodity economy. Eliminating self-consciousness. Tartar woman in Afghan army suit. Saying she always thinking of herself as man. Bribing priest to marry her to her wife—at age fourteen. At twenty wife dying. She miserable for a while. Finding herself another. But problems—likely due to Tartar blood. She'd be happiest as master of harem. Also super-femme dope-dyke in Moscow prison. Gorgeous unabashed disaster. And half-Jewish half-Romany singer. What intensity. Romanticism of utter resistance!

Out for last métro. Train rumbling through abandoned station. Makeshift bed on darkened platform. Garbage bags. A sheet. Shuddering at rats. Soon coming out. Smartest of creatures. According to homeless paper. When stealing egg. One lying back. Holding egg in paws. While accomplice pulling him by tail. Shuddering at imagination required. To survive. For SDFs, homeless. Or any minor culture.

96. Earlier again impression being watched. By faces in store across street. At least two. Staring steadily. Finally crossing for a look. Turning out to be only those framed dressed-up dogs. On wall behind windows. Some trick of light. Dogs in business suits. Dogs as judges. Plus one bourgeois Victorian dog woman. All brown and lugubrious. Making me want face cream.

Face burning with eczema.

Crossing little park. Mad blind woman on bench. "Watching" with whites of eyes. Entering Bon Marché. Full of women. In tailored suits (uniforms). Twice trying tester of Christian Dior lipstick. No. 436. Pair of purple plaid gloves. Paris-funk. Don't buy. Don't buy face cream. Being unsure what kind. Stepping out door on side. Facial splotches muted. In darkness of boutique windows. Giving aura of flowers. Painted as if under water. Porous. Ambiguous. Entering traiteur. Patronne behind cash. Moving jowls. This way and that. Because foreigner taking too long. Getting money out. For simple pain, bread. I therefore quickly adding pâté aux prunes. To commande, order. At $25 per pound: good for the blood. Now it's oui Madame. Non Madame. Au plaisir Madame. Behind her—employee. African-French. White assistant's hat. Asking Monsieur-le-patron for raise. Keeping his dignity. Though manifestly furious. Because patron barely listening.

Large family dog moving closer. Closer. Growling.


97. Raining. Entering café lit by giant geometric teardrops. Suspended from ceiling. Smaller wall versions. Over curly-pawed tables. Pretty but unheated. So sitting far from window. R arriving almost simultaneously. *Le Nouvel Obs* in hand. On cover *Fifteen Leading Intellectuals.* Derrida. Lyotard. Deleuze. Etc. All worriedly reflecting on growing entrenchment of Right. Which Right they having spent lives striving to philosophically defeat. By *en principe* displacing. Deferring. Huge Western *I.* Casting unecological shadow. Over earth. Malheureusement issue not including Kristeva. Weil. Arendt. Irigary. Buci-Glucksmann. Collin. Wittig. Nor any other woman.

105

Maybe women too busy with 1000 little details. To be seen as *truly* philosophical. I ironizing to R. Nodding at several pointed bras. Under well-pressed sweaters. À la mode again. The shape of women's silhouettes. Expressing something of epoch. Crinoline for imperialist expansion. Or "sadistic" bloomers (B saying). At outset of suffragettes. R agreeing feminine. In Paris. Considered dangerous. Therefore requiring effort to contain. Through discipline of hyper-female roles. Albeit he protesting men *also* wearing perfume. Carrying purses. Then smiling fake embarrassed. With pleasant friendly mouth. Of guy from Winnipeg.

Suddenly beggar's neat dark jacket. Pushed up against café window. Cars piling on sidewalk. Making way for loud demonstration. Female café patrons. Turning gazes perpetually bemused. To prevent unpleasant wrinkles. At angry crowd winding up Rennes. On way to prime minister's. Chanting against layoffs. I telling R demos increasing. Weekly under studio window. Contained by hordes of riot cops. Further. On subject of containment. Of feminine. I offering as trope. Little grey carefully fenced-in alley. Burgeoning with roses. Seen recently. On Revolution's anniversary. Off monumental Panthéon square. Where HOMME or homonym inscribed on all façades. Countless roses also strewn. Between Panthéon's citation-Roman columns. By women. Demonstrating. In memory of Revolutionary heroine Olympe de Gouges. Singing: *Put Olympe in the Panthéon! / Marie Curie too! / Hey hey in democracy / Women count too.*

Walking up Raspail. Still wondering if seeming disregard of women intellectuals. Implying conscious or unconscious resistance of weight. Of feminine. In culture. Boulevard wide and cold. In autumn wind and rain. Gertrude Stein calling this patch. Retreat from Moscow. In studio. Pouring glass of rouge. B falling open at passage. Citing a dandy: *It is I who invented the fashion of facial tics. Currently replaced by the monocle. The tic involved closing the eye with a certain movement of mouth and bearing. An elegant man ought always to have something convulsive or nervy about him. Which others may impute to his natural devilishness, or to the fever of passion, or to anything they want.*

98. Ages since writing. Earlier. Stepping out. Brisk. Partly cloudy. Red jeans. Scooped top with braid around edges. Blazer. Rather French profile. Therefore stopping to take picture. In hair salon façade mirror. While 20th. In form of automobile. Racing over backdrop. Plus drunk. Asleep on median strip. Grey-flannelled leg hooked around bench's iron back. Also wearing blazer. Well-cut grey hair. Rather elegant profile. But head cushioned on greasy khaki knapsack. Maybe wanting to be alone. Or casualty of alcoholism. Losing job. Evicted from little room. No use trying to live here on less than $4,000 a month. Mayor of Paris declaring.

Continuing up Rennes. Dodging little Saabs and Renaults. Loving walking here. Sun alternately streaming. Obliterating physiognomies. No longer nouns. But movement. Disappearing. Now heavily raining. Sitting out anyway. Over drain smelling of beer. Cold air blowing up. Under chair. From labyrinthine grottoes. Métro. Sewers. Fetid breath of Paris. Two cold coffees. Watching shadows lengthening. On la Gaîté opposite. Where Colette once performing. Having walked in old boots across city. Drawing mole above lip. Rice-powdering delicious arms. Paris a drug. P saying on phone. Yes Paris a drug. A woman. And I waking this a.m. Thinking there must be some way. Of staying. Now my love's silhouette of rooftops eclipsing. Into night. Cold heinous breath. Blowing on privates. Through grille underneath.

Light streaming across table. Café doors open. But how come *no square of chocolate*. On saucer by graceful little cup. With CAFÉ DE LA PLACE written on it. Though others getting one. Therefore summoning woman waiter (rare sight in Paris). Who redheaded. Like redheaded woman. Seen earlier in basement. Scrubbing dishes. Next to urinoir with piece of crystal in it. Barman redheaded too. Place likely owned by family. Working. Working. Coordinating gestures. To tune of some inner familial melody. Conjuring utopist Fourier's dream. Of republic. Wherein workers. B saying. Choreographed like opera. Every gesture efficient. Because marking time of music. Waiter taking out pen on chain. From black vest of Pariswaiter uniform. Worn for centuries. And noting "chocolate" down. It occurring to me. Fourier's utopia. With everyone marching in tune with everybody else. Living in lookalike tenements in lookalike arcades. Too much like Poe's lookalike crowd.

Fax from Z. Written from second-storey bar. Chez nous. Where she serving afternoon tequilas. Looking out on giant TV saucer. Describing smell of street after rain. People walking ankle-deep in water. Against wind. When suddenly a shot. Cops. Wounding Haitian taxi driver. "Mistaken identity."

99. On TV—terrifying documentary about "soldiers of fortune." Young men from all over. Coming to fight on any paying side. In ex-Yugoslavia. Mostly English-speaking. From white working classes of Britain. Ireland. Also from Australia. For the money. Liking their "work." They not calling it that. No concept of any side being particularly right. Something to do. Saying one with Cockney accent. Shaved head. Keeps me outta trouble.

Z also joining brigade: work group for Cuba. Reason partly political. Likewise no good jobs. For youth.

100. Café Saint-Germain. Asian tourists drinking tea. Lovely skin. Clouds like high fog. With single ray of light. Passing through. Exhaling milky breath. I sniffing espresso. Thinking how I increasingly aroused. Before sleeping. Causing dreams wildly erotic. Last one slightly troubling. Someone wanting to prepare long piece of T's shoulder. In exquisite way. For me. First consulting butcher. Deboned. I thinking would be nice. Rolled in herbs. Then thinking of Grand Palais yesterday. Whose glass-and-iron roof. Often spied. Glinting from Pont-Neuf. Malheureusement up close. Palais façade *academic*. Arts and sciences marching over. In mythological tropes. Basin with sylphs. Angels. Pineapples. Horses. Prancing towards pont Alexandre-III's ornate pillories with golden-winged steeds. Golden alley. Rolling towards Napoléon's gold-leafed tomb. Behind Invalides. Opposite.

All this to avoid. Describing singular *L'Âme au corps, Body and Soul* exhibition. Within. Affecting. Like no other. As if wandering on edge of uncanny. Or in Dr. Freud's atelier. Where "one" confronting past (unconscious). In form of androids with beaks for noses. Pointed ears of rats. Chins of dogs. Or inversely. Animals sporting human features. Humanfaced silken baboons. Or organic. Meeting inorganic. In de Grandville's cartoon-faced flowers. Presaging advertising. B saying. Or Wiertz's Rosine. Chatting nonchalantly with skeleton. Segueing on through early instruments. Of medicine. Or torture (indistinguishable). Toward room where early photo technology. Joining early psychoanalysis. In murals of countless tiny mug shots. "Representing" criminal "types." Interpolated in "oriental" fold of eye. Sloping forehead. Pointy teeth. Signalling untoward animal instincts. Nineteenth passion for technology. Frequently leading to premature (reactionary) synthesis. But also to Redon's unfathomable watery painted figures. Sliding out of gaze. Or to Courbet's sleep investigations. Two fabulous naked women slumbering. In each other's arms. The whole sublimated. Analyzed. Summed up in little captions. Projecting: 19th-century subject. Waking post-Commune. Doubting reliability of species. Which doubt fostering "modern" psychiatric ward. Wherein master himself pacing. Narrating someone else's dreams. They being someone else's: impossible to pin down. Resultant shock. To ordered 19th-century mind. Ultimately spawning surrealism.

And "one" walking there near cusp of 21st. Mid countless objects representing point of convergence. Between 19th and 20th. Feeling certain—with hindsight—of genius. It being task of museum to make "one" feel lucid. Grizzled feast having been laid out for "one's" unique consumption. Each item. Tagged with orchestrated (unconscious) association. By aura-conjuring hand of curator. Therefore—racing towards Champs-Élysées. In dark. (Days being extremely short now.) Feeling certain marvellous to be had. Rows and rows of cops. Blocking boulevard. Probably another demonstration. Home on bus. Knees pressed against those of bourgeoise. On narrow facing seats. Clearly disapproving. Of straggly North American hair. Very short lashes.

101. Nearly 4:45. Crossing Luxembourg. Hoping black crowd of clouds. Soon releasing few blessed rays of eczema-salving sun. But already tree silhouettes. Raising nearly leafless arms. Against paling sky. Ponds at their feet. Woman with bare leg bleeding. Above rolled-down stockings. Suddenly turning. Toothless. And asking for cigarette. I grabbing broken clasp of knapsack. Shaking head. A *lie!* Odour of musty rotting leaves. Rising up. Earlier smelled in dream. Wherein I living in house. Needing fumigation. Given pipes leading in full of rhinoceros. Or hippopotami. Or some huge lizard. Also starlings—this most frightening—in garret. But house not really belonging to me. Dream title: *I Am Not Responsible.* Turning right on Raspail. Masses of students. In brightly coloured clothes. Coming up behind. From suburban lycées. Many Arab-French. Chanting *Une deux trois générations. On s'en fout. Nous sommes chez nous, First second third generation. Who cares. We're from here.* P banging on studio door. Looking more geometric than ever. Angles protruding in clinging knit dress. Hair standing up. Dusky cheekbones. Flushed from excitement of taunting cops. In demo below. Young Neo-Situationist in tow. Loose white shirt. Bow-tie. Carrying roll of posters on which painted: RIONS ENSEMBLE DE NOTRE INCONSCIENT. Immediate intense conversation. He displaying charm. Of well-bred son of French mother. I.e. knowing how to play junior artist. To my senior one. Saying French too nuts about technique. Surface. Shaking curly head. Saying he really tired. Of bourgeoisie. Periodically checking out window. To see if motorized toilet. Still chained to side of bus stop. To crap in the street. He laughing. Meaning: like cars. P watching our absorbed conversation. Feigning jealousy. Time to go she saying suddenly. Loudly. Putting on coat. Turning head to add.

Wouldn't it be tragic. If he hit by a bus.


102. Trying gathering at embassy. Walking over in muggy steel-grey air. Having showered for second time. Pressed red jeans. Polished boots. Pressed very clean sweater. Red lipstick matching watchband. One colour detail picking up another. Ordinary apparel thus

signing "outfit." Funeral cloud heavy with storm. Lowering through window of winding stairs. Climbing to elegant pastel room. Where young filmmaker being fêted. Standing in middle of circle. Suave designer linen jacket. Gorgeous redheaded wife. With "latest production." Strapped to chest. Embassy wives and female staff stepping forward. Gooh-ing and gah-ing. Wife possibly bending frame a little. Bouncing kid up and down too vigorously.

Or is this dance of devotion part of her success. In periods of decadence dances often pushed to their limit. Traditional quadrille thus becoming can-can. The Latin two-step resuscitating. One millennium later. For nostalgic youth in search of delusions. The tango. Re-abandoning melodrama. Accumulated mid-century. In ballrooms of Europe. Suddenly letting loose again. Foxtrot. Stiffening to goosestep. Under conditions of economic retrenchment. Currently being signalled at bar. By white-gloved waiter bringing out. Only one bottle. At time.

T and I dancing pas-de-deux. To neighbouring empty pastel room. Unfurnished. Due to cutbacks. Having failed to be noticed. Despite T's flaming outfit. Despite our having added loud baby-loving comments. To cacophony. True—star himself affording us a word. Leaning forward. Momentarily confiding. In totally disarming manner. That notwithstanding all those postmodern theories. About his work. His ideas really simple. Just telling stories. I protesting "one" *admiring* his success. At playing line between experimentation and narrative. Compared to "one's" own.

His eyes clouding over.

But T suddenly hailing. Long silver woman. Recently seen waving. From Marais café window. Currently preparing to climb winding staircase. At end of our pastel retreat. In slender skirt and little high-heeled boots. Foot with fake military strap round ankle. Pausing mi-glissade. To answer offhandedly T's fake question. Re: recessionary art policies. Then T and I retreating. Out embassy door. Marching up rue de Constantine. Golden dome of Napoléon's tomb glowing behind. T hissing: if we just a *little* better known. They falling all over us.

Air thick and damp. We climbing to second floor of Saint-Germain. Eating steak/frites. Bad onion gravy. Acidy red wine. T unimpressed. Looking up at citation art-nouveau lampshades. Down at brass bar. With sworly mother-of-pearl inset. Saying she tired of overworn tropes. Daddy. Mommy. Baby. I arguing cosiness of 19th. What people *mostly* missing. In 20th. Plus time. To dream. To wander. She replying honey. Of which class you speaking.

103. Now in window across street. Two men in tuxes sitting. Civilized. Quiet. Facing each other. Waiting. Waiting. *I* waiting. To see if winning tiny literary award. For which nommée. Waiting for British editor. Waiting for French agent. Waiting—

When below window. Appearing man in feudal outfit. Sitting on slow horse. Led by two other men. In red-belted singlets. Green tights. Little bells. Passing. Likely an advertisement. Then a shout. And demo of unemployed workers. Surging up street. Loose trousers. Sagging bellies. Passing. Quickly. Efficiently. Silence. Boulevard eerily empty. Then from somewhere indeterminate. Terrific African-sounding music. By time I in street. Lycéen(ne)s again. Fresh. Energetic. Stepping rhythmically. To mesmerizing beat. Lead bongos. Played by young Caucasian. Face fierce. Intense. Caught up in total mood. Noticing I watching. He allowing small smile. Worker from other now-dispersed unemployment demo. Saying proudly: my daughter in there.

Silence again.

Yet a third demo coming. Also playing music. World beat maybe. But as they moving closer. *Their* huge banner saying BEAUJOLAIS NOUVEAU. This being day the new wine coming out. Tonight—fêtes in many bistros and cafés. ALL NIGHT GUINGUETTE I seeing earlier. On swag. On barrel. At Edgar-Quinet. Vaguely thinking of going. Imagining music of accordions. Women in high heels. Slingback straps. Shortish haircuts. Rouge and cheap lipstick. Covering fatigue of long day at work. Men with small pots. Slightly red noses. Uppity new wine speeding up system. Relentless gaiety. In bracing fall air.

Calling R. Saying I hoping rising energy in streets—like Breton's poet with revolver—about to cause explosion. He suggesting supper in worker-run restaurant. Near south periphery. Where waiters still called comrade. Under dusty railway overpass. Turning night. Onto rue de la Butte-aux-Cailles, Quail-Ridge Street. Air of Paris suddenly fresh and quiet. Stucco former country houses. Drunk exiting from bakery. Waving stolen loaf. Boulangère's sad gaze in window. Toward LES TEMPS DES CERISES. After old Commune song: *I'll always like cherry blossom time / it's that particular spring that stays in my heart / an open wound / even Lady Fortune if offered to me / will never heal my pain.*

Inside little tables with white paper tablecloths. Socialists in shirtsleeves. Or synthetic cardigans. Chatting optimistically. Huge mural of cut-out workers against blackboard background. Simulating Le Sueur's watercoloured cutouts of citoyens and citoyennes. Against blue sky. At time of Revolution. Shelves against mirrors. Empty wine bottles. All shapes and sizes. Squarefaced guy at cash. Waiter ponytailed and ruddy. Turning sideways. And flicking cockroach. R politely pointing out. From breadbasket. Then implying we hysterical. Or lacking solidarity. Ordering salt beef. From cheaper menu. R also ordering stuffed crab vol-au-vent entrée. Swimming in floury alleged asparagus sauce. He nearly spitting out. Two guys beside. Possibly Arab-French. Speaking of Bosnia.

Back under overpass. R saying restaurant better in '70s. When worker solidarity bearing prouder standards. Now no aura of seamless perfection. One expecting from good French cooking. On métro—group of young artists. Complaining about difficulty of finding studios. À Paris on évacue le peuple et les artistes, in Paris we evict artists and the people. Saying pale bespectacled youth. Voice rising rhetorically. To girl. With gorgeous black curls.

104. Raising store. Still grey and foggy. Heaviness in air. Dressing. Creeping past concierge's door. Avoiding interception. Stepping into street. Nice smell of mist. Almost choked by diesel. Trace of all those damp autumn days. Of different cities lived in. Black

wool leggings. Black wool sweater. Blousy jacket over. Simultaneously "in." And "classical." Feeling—suddenly—endlessly re-
newable. Unfortunately aging skin-yellowed-from-cirrhosis waiter
in cheap café round corner. Refusing to serve espresso. It being
lunch. Smelling of cabbage. I in turn refusing to leave. Boots out-
stretched among mégots on tiles. Opening B at *Prostitution* section. Describing feminine "fauna" of declining passages. Using tones
of possibly suspect fascination. In way he abutting grisettes. Lifting skirts to make ends meet. At end of factory shift. On elderly
"witch-like" used-clothing ladies. Plus *"Glovers"*—*his* emphasis.
Which suspect fascination he immediately "dialectically" diffus-
ing. By naming one more (earlier) passage "creature": *les Demoi-
selles*. Term applied to male incendiaires, subversives. Dressed as
women. Frequenting arcades. Ca 1830.

"One" experiencing similar fascination. Watching famous
brothel madame. On TV talk show later. Firm mouth and neck of
man. Unbelievable silky skin though nearly seventy. Blonde-sil-
very helmet. Saying oh she never beautiful enough to be prostitute
herself. Mais non her girls very happy. Successful. Among her ex's—
three marquises. Wives of bankers. Politicians. But she won't
breathe another word. Non. No longer in business. Too much
changed due to drugs. AIDS. Agreeing graciously to fake contest.
Showing what it takes. No candidates over twenty-two please. Too
set in ways.

Three hopefuls stepping up from audience. Eyes struggling
between taking this as joke. And wanting to win. Two out at once
for overlarge hips. The third tall. Skinny. Would do if a nose job.
Smile of pride playing on her lips. Madame Claude normally also
examining breasts. Not here of course. And. Let me see your purse.
Flinging it petulantly on floor. Contents spilling out. One hair in
comb. Make-up loose in bottom. Instead of neatly arranged. In
impeccable little case. And you out on your ear.

105. *"Fascination"* bis
    Last night—LES FOLIES BERGÈRE! Name meaning—I at first
thinking—one shepherdess/many follies. But more likely after small

114

hotel passage—Cité-Bergère, Shepherd's Village. Anyway—never realizing how mad the French. To point of cruel. T and I giggling. Even as we sitting. At "Maria Callas" riding bicycle. Round three beefcake angels. Bare feet. Boxer shorts. Wings. Perching nonchalantly on packing-box homes. I.e. she dead. Then transluscent-skinned "Marie-Antoinette." Sauntering across stage. In nothing (but heels and crown). Claiming clothes stolen in métro. Behind her on cloud: several space cadets. "Billie Holiday." Dragging half-extenuated body. Across floor. The whole punctuated by rows of can-can dancing women. Powdered skin and tiaras. Froufrous. High high heels. Disappointingly tame. I nearly standing. Screaming *take it off*. In Protestant voyeuristic way. But distracted. Or distanced. By tiny man in drag. Throwing up legs. In front centre row of luscious lovelies.

Maybe this why theatre nearly empty. Maybe "one"—having come for sex—resenting ravaged drag queen. Singing "Is That All There Is?" So thin the word AIDS etching frame around her. Or Tunisian performer. Allegedly "discovered" singing in métro (homeless theme again). Huge guitar and short bellbottoms. Belting out "Baby, *Sht-a-a-and* By Me." Two Godots. Cracking homeless jokes. In packing-box shelters. While feathered sequined dancers. Leading beefcake angel. Across background. On string.

T and I still giggling. Scurrying out through painted-on decor. Of turquoise Folies' foyer. Turquoise painted canapés. Gold painted prancing pony. Chandelier on back. A few diners leaving little rooms. Having drunk overpriced champagne. While raising social conscience. Through frosted doors of Folies' façade. Still giggling. Hurrying towards métro. By Notre-Dame-de-Lorette. Just below Pigalle. Which church's brass/scarlet/frosted glass interior. More apropos of ballroom. Than of temple. According to B. "Lorette" in 19th having become term for fallen woman. Past some of those racing cafés. Typical in neighbourhood. With bookies. Dangerous dogs. Where earlier seeing modest couple. Impeccable young wife in pressed jeans. Cheap blazer. Likely spotless nylon things under. Smoking husband. Plus in-laws. Eating bad frites. Quartier darker than others. Drunk swaggering out in front.

Funny thing about travelling. Emerging métro du Bac. Onto windy Raspail. I thinking *not* of Folies Bergère. Or beauties. But of modest wife. In restaurant window. "Ordinary" when travelling. Often seeming *in relief*. Whereas "ordinary." Chez nous. By dint of repetition. Forever fading. Toward banality of background.

106. Café below Panthéon. Maurice Chevalier crooning sentimental tune. On radio. Now "Baby You Talk Too Much" coming over airwaves. Then French ballad. Vaguely political. Conferring certain majestic atmosphere. Maybe Ferrat. Singing solidarity. Or surrealist Aragon's dithyrambic love poems. To Elsa. *C'est si peu dire que je t'aime,* it's so little to say I love you. A grand amour— Luxembourg newspaper vendor saying. Redfaced. Peaked cap. Playing tape on little portable. Eyes floating towards ceiling. Of small kiosque. Extraordinaire. An example for all of us. Naturellement not mentioning. Aragon's "extra" extraordinary loves: boys.

So nice to sit. Not having to go anywhere tonight. To meet anyone. Soon back to studio. Passing large jellied trout. In traiteur window. Near Gertrude Stein's. Whose genius. Being American. Interested in gathering what ordinary (common). In all of "us." While loving Paris as refuge. Of individuals (artists). Traces of winter. In air. Ankle-high in pamphlets. From yet another unemployment demonstration. Man. Writing *Je suis sans travail. Sans abri,* I am jobless. Homeless. Rewinding long scarf around neck. Waving complicitly at marchers. Rushing up Saint-Placide. Shouting *Pas-de-licenciements.* Green city cleaners. Bringing up rear. No—last contingent riot police. Waiting parked in large buses along sidewalk. Bristling with Christmas decorations. Tasteful. Restrained. I.e. bereft of tinsel. Flashing lights. Emphasis on red velvet ribbons turning storefronts into packages. Huge tree in front of Hôtel Lutétia. Replacing oyster stand.

But first. Little more nodding in steam from coffee. Pedestrians rushing by outside. Scarves wrapped artfully. Round chilly necks.

Ballad over. Familiar rolling québécois accent at bar. Boasting it minus forty chez nous. Reinforcing image. Conferred by Voltaire: le Canada nothing, rien. But 100 acres. Of snow.

107. Across the street mannequins *not* in tuxes. As appearing from distance. But in black wide-lapelled suits. White shirts. Still sitting civilized. In anticipation of coming fêtes. One with leg crossed. Foot on pile of dirty discarded magazines. Put out. For garbage. Homeless theme once more.

Walking through gardens. Today benches empty. French "winter" snow. Sticking to leaves remaining on trees. Gulls taking polar dips. Off stiff edge of ice. Stepping up. Jumping off again. Still-flaming asters. Mums. Zinnias. Cascading from cement bowls on cement balustrade. Curving around pond basin. Providing only colour. Out other gate. Crossing Gertrude Stein's street. Thinking how narrator. In century of automobile. Necessarily nomadic. Yet fatalement distanced from other nomads going by window. Such as now: on TV. Seemingly *most* tragic group of homeless. Still employed but unable to afford room. In extravagantly priced Paris. Thus living in rat-infested caves. Along walls of Seine. Camera zooming in. Guy crawling at night under threadbare blankets. Shoes neatly polished. Pants neatly folded. On hanger on nail. Hammered into stone. Needing to sleep in order to keep working. Clinging to last semblance of normality. Before falling off edge.

Watching—it occurring to me. SDFs figuring continually in media here. While in Americas. Where surely more numerous. Homeless only occasionally selected. As subject of reportage. After which: "old news." Trick of continual fake renewal. First used by great journalist Mussolini. Whose government—according to B—running like tabloid. Serving up one main sensation per day. Whereas French media using other approach entirely: ritualistically mirroring good republican consciousness. E.g. now on TV news. Minister proudly announcing opening of *day-time* drop-in centres. For showering and drinking coffee. Before stepping out again. Appropriateness of this. Reflected in enthusiasm of reporter's voice. Likely ancien soixante-huitard, May '68er. Later. Coming up Rennes. Same good consciousness. Seen in bourgeoisie. Quite hysterical. Hands folded. Good blue suit. Trying to get young Romany beggar mother. And two babies. To go home with her.

Snowing in Sarajevo.

117

108. Yesterday visiting *three* of those old commercial passages or arcades. B calling Ur-forms of 20th. Presaging shopping malls. As fussily intimate. As old régime interiors. On entering—getting sense for first time—of 19th living conditions. Eternal cold and dankness rising up from tiles. Under grey light. From overhead sooty glass-and-iron roof. Filtering melancholy. That "humour" of 19th. Con-temporaneously treated as pathological. People sitting in small cosy-looking-but-in-reality-unheated. Boutiques and offices. Wearing scarves and jackets. On awaking this a.m. Chill and swollen eye.

It being fêtes. Already pseudo-Victorian atmosphere. Along boulevards. Leisure-class women. In longish tailored coats. Run-ning in and out of pine-decked beribboned grands magasins, de-partment stores. Students with painted faces. Dispensing flyers. Chestnuts being roasted. By man in blue turban. Boulevard's clear wide vista. Having cut through neighbourhoods. After 1848 re-bellion. Almost to Arc de Triomphe. Providing wide panoptic per-spective. As in "wild west" city. B saying. Rendering dark arcades dated. Ultimately even ploughing over passage de l'Opéra. Aragon loving so much. With baths. For making love. Specialty boutiques. Offering Calvados. Hernia bandages. Porto. Dog and puppy bis-cuits.

Anyway coming down Haussmann. Windy as chez nous. Shivering. Despite leather jacket. Over heavy sweater. Under blue short man's raincoat. Entering café. Fog falling outside café win-dow. Faint view of buildings. Climbing up Montmartre. Like im-pressionistic painting. Which Belle Époque ambience further fos-tered. By moustachioed café patrons. White shirts. Vestons. Sip-ping Pernod. Then out again. Past scaffolded façade. Of PASSAGE DES PRINCES. Renovated to virtual-reality arcade. Featuring holo-graphs. Robots. Cyberboats. Neuron nests. Marking end of time as we knowing it.

Right on Montmartre. Into narrow still intact early 19th PAS-SAGE DES PANORAMAS. Faded curved corridor. Silver palm branches. Meeting in middle. Disappointed eye. Taking in cemented-over floor mosaics. In front of boutique entrances. Effacing names of original proprictors. Only GRAVEUR STERN DEPUIS 1840 still writ in tiny tiles. Before door of Stern family business. Also painted-over wood-carved or metalwork boutique façades. Separated by yellow marble columns. Running up between. Though pretty Salon du Thé. Maintaining original floral wood-finished front. Where long skirts or redingotes of early 19th Parisians. Coming to escape mud. Racket. Of narrow streets outside. Relaxing behind newspapers. Before shopping for tobacco. Perfumes. Cashmere shawls from imperially exotic Egypt. Or stepping into panoramas or rotundas. On each side of passage entrance. Which rotundas. Wrapping spectator round in painted scenes of history. Womb-like. Secure. Making one feel present. Yet at safe distance. From some famous battle. Or invention.

Exiting. Crossing boulevard Montmartre. Entering PASSAGE JOUFFROY. Mocking faces of MUSÉE GRÉVIN, wax museum, window. Staring cheerily at passers. Strolling toward huge clock at end of hall. With HÔTEL CHOPIN written under. Male couple coming out. Corridor jogging left. Past poster shops. Gay postcards. Stamps. Engravings. Kept by idealists left over from '70s. Smoking. Freezing. Beyond Jouffroy. More obscure PASSAGE VERDEAU. Surreal mannequin head on awning. Same outdated objects. Stamps. Presses. Secondhand cameras. Same restaurant cold and dampness. These labyrinths. Jogging to left. To right. In muddling 19th-century way. Like train. Like English way of thinking. Gertrude Stein saying.

109. Yesterday using carrot of charming young waiters. Serving apéritifs. In clinging overalls. In passage Jouffroy. For luring R to Grévin wax museum.

Unfortunately on way over. Doing stupid thing. Like in Palais-Royal garden. When that kid shiny with hunger. Asking for money. Now a guy in métro du Bac. Seeking signatures on petition for orphans from "the south." Little heads. Lined up in photo. I saying can't. Given petition requiring address. Keep repeating can't. Guy staring. Incredulously.

Grévin a scream. Distorting mirrored labyrinth. Presenting history backwards. Modern retreating toward mediaeval. Starting off with Fonda. In *Barbarella* space suit. Surprised multiple orgasm expression of '60s film. On physiognomy. Michael Jackson moonwalking. Backwards. Towards Communards. Napoléons. Jacobins. Several Louis. And queens. "All history" being laid out for consumption. Of panopticon eye. I.e. assuming "we" seeing it all the same. Little dauphin. Dying in little cell. While rats eating food. Little wax face terrified and feverish. Head of some noble on pole. Being waved by victorious sans-culotte at incestuous lesbian Marie-Antoinette's window. She falling naturellement in faint. Pallor of sculpting material. Painted. Giving almost cartoon effect. For contemporary viewer. Who further aware. Head of one hero often replaced by another. On reclad body. According to vicissitudes of public opinion. Labyrinth ending in Palais des Mirages. Small room. Belle Époque. Columns entwined with snakes. Masks. Lights going out. Darkness slowly filling with lit-up butterflies. And stars. Stiffly rising. Descending. On faintly visible wires. "Beautiful." But technology so dated. Being chiefly conceived. Like old panoramas. For spectators. Watching from immoveable centre.

Happily—I distracted by R's pleasure in glimmering tight-jeaned ass of young man. Commenting—as we exiting—that arcade life reviving. Compared to first visit twenty years back. Young man heading for Hôtel Chopin. Through open door. We glimpsing dark pink lobby. Campy lampshades. Men coming down stairs. We entering café with real wicker chairs. Opposite Grévin. With handsome male waiters. Little red kerchiefs knotted round necks. To drink fine porto. Out of lovely porto glasses. Beige palm trees in relief. Climbing up beige wall. R taking in male fauna. I the porto. Sinking by osmosis. Into roof of mouth.

110. Every morning wakened by neighbour's door slamming. The duchess I thinking. Imagining magnificent fur coat. She wearing since temperature dropped to 30s. Going out for bread. But just

120

the help arriving. New maid this morning. Bread under arm. Knocking on studio by mistake. Falling back asleep. Getting up dissatisfied.

One more walk in Luxembourg. Pond basin red-ribboned off. Due to mud. This walk always improving mood. Passing statues of old French queens. Jogging dream. To surface. Driving in back of car. Four women in front. Wispy haircuts. Hoop earrings. High cheekbones. Thin but muscular backs in striped shirts or white clinging tops. Slit-up long tight sleeves. With little silver knobs or buttons. Then realizing they French drag queens. This making me happy. Though they ignoring or unaware. I sitting behind.

Now glued to seat of café. At Edgar-Quinet. If staying. Should be looking for work. Apartment. Instead—sitting. Hugging usual grey white light. Around me. Watching sky. Behind unusual hotel façade. On other corner of square. Three tiers of shutters. Magnificent. Big black cloud. Pink and grey fringed. Dressy as the Opéra. Moving forward. Back. Like divagations of Proustian sentence. Which divagations preventing premature (biased) synthesis. By leading toward multiple conclusions . . . *Plunged into an agitated somnambulence, my adolescence enveloped everything with the same dream in the quartier in which it strolled, and it never occurred to me that there could be an 18th-century building in rue Royale, not to mention my astonishment, had I learned that porte Saint-Martin and porte Saint-Denis, chefs-d'oeuvre of the time of Louis XIV, were not contemporary with the more recent buildings in these sordid neighbourhoods* . . . Embroidering sadness with pleasures of existence. French way of absorbing melancholy. E.g. shop window next to men's boutique. Full of treated real roses. In picture frames. Or in perfect round little everlasting bouquets. Of type monsieur taking mademoiselle in old French movies. Embalmed to never fade.

111. *"L'Avant-garde"*

Grey as usual. Black soot creeping in around casement windows. Papers scattered. Reams of curly fax pages. Filling corners.

Also growing chaos in street. Last night explosive demo. Nearly making me miss *avant-garde party*. At last invited to! Having run down for bottle of Vittel. Barricades everywhere. Rows and rows of cops. Helmets. Sticks. Raised. Pavés flying. Cops' ranks growing thicker. Preventing marchers from approaching nearby ministerial buildings. And me from returning. Chez moi.

Therefore deciding to take quartier from behind. Via métro. Heart beating madly. Though *naturellement* solidaire. Train completely empty. Some striking teachers jumping on. As I jumping off. Union look. Duffel coats. Scraggly hair. Waterbottles. Drooping placards. Sheepish grins. Trying to get back into mêlée. Nostalgic for '60s. Like soixante-huitard businessman on TV. Earlier. Dragging bags along highway. During airport bus strike. Are you mad at the workers. Small smirk in camera. Non—it reminds me of mai '68.

Finally reaching studio. Via tiny rue de la Chaise. Angling round courtyard. Squeezing by water trucks and cleaners. Concierge opening door. Having locked to keep fugitives out. Practically welcoming in arms. Running up stairs. Looking out studio window. Noticing pavé-throwers inching backward. Then suddenly street normal. Spotless.

Running out once more. Green silk knit top. Stretched ruffly at bottom. Instead of de rigueur black. Taking bus south. Crossing boulevard near periphery. As wide as in L.A. Dwarfing little kiosques. Café-tabacs. Hotdog stands. Video arcades. Second bus heading through semi-industrial neighbourhood. Street very dark. Climbing to upper floor. Of rather rundown building. Ringing any door. Stressed man answering. Curly-headed kid clinging. Fearfully to leg. Pointing to renovated foundry. Below.

Ringing again. Slender '70s-style woman. Helmet of platinum. Answering. White walls. Gas fireplaces. Low tables. Laden with flowers. Tomatoes/mozzarella. Eggs. Bread. Wine. People around long oval table. Arranged in little groups. Men. Wine-red of face. Otherwise fit. Hennaed older females. Friendly to each other. Younger women avoiding elder women's proximity. As if fearing contamination. Preferring hovering on borders of older male constellations. Though one youngish woman. In black plastic pantsuit. Sitting apart. Suddenly launching into witty impersonation. Of dead Oulipolian Perec. Ruffling up her hair. Cigarette in lips. Expression mi-figue mi-raisin, sheepish. Eliciting brief appreciative smiles. From older guys opposite. Conversation quickly resuming.

I slipping into empty chair. Beside her. After a while she saying—confidentially—she writing experimental prose. In evenings. But throwing out daily. I saying oh no. Old guilt returning. For having written nothing. In leisure lottery studio. She kindly pointing out *la Pléiade* editor. Plus secretary of Mittérand. Pince nez and striped shirt. Poet Hocquard.

112. Across street now two mannequins. In exquisite black leather jackets. Over well-cut suits. Standing in field of sparsely sown apples. On window in white script a "poem." Dead words. Such spaces between. Impossible to remember.

Day also vacuous. Having missed final chance. To sit under Chagall's floating ceiling. Depicting seven famous libretti. In shockingly extravagant Second Empire Opéra building. Overplastered. With oeils-de-boeuf. Masks. Busts. Etc. Conceived as distraction. From terror. Monotony. Of pre-Commune period. Métro from du Bac. Under Seine. Via Solferino. Assemblée Nationale. Already feeling nostalgic. Unfortunately getting held up near Madeleine. Announcement on intercom. Voyageur malade. Euphemism. For someone jumping on tracks. In next station. Bad drunk with cut-up face. Leaping on train. Fleeing cops. Screaming les pédés, queers get aid. SDFs, homeless get aid. HIV-positives get aid. And I getting nothing. *Mais je vais me défendre,* I'm going to show them. Barrelling down car. Asking for money. To each man refusing. Shouting *Je vais t'enculer,* I'm going to assfuck you.

But opera tickets costing more than food for week.

113. Just before bed. Interview on TV with Fellini. We sharing birthdays. Big man. Climbing in car. Being chauffeured across city. Only deciding what to film on way to set. Saying artist needing to be totally disponible. To creative process. I thinking: mystical but

true. E.g. in Paris "one" totally disponible. *If* having equivalent of leisure lottery studio. Providing space for thinking. So ego blossoming to point of (almost) overcoming guilt (fear). No longer desiring punishment. Which desire earlier causing terrible paranoia re: authorities. Now only being punished. By imminent departure.

After which—predictably—*"Departure Dream."* Wherein I on canapé with québécois successor. To studio. He taking hold of nose. But in nice way. Twisting back head. And kissing me. Penetrating deeply. Nice strong prick having condom on it. An old radical. Possibly sympathizer of Félquistes, Québec Liberation Front. Or else radical anarchist theatre group. Breaking everything. Until house (loft or studio). Having little furniture left. And I finding myself walking. Along road in Québec countryside. Some nice fish visible on surface of lake.

Fish visible on surface of lake. Are dead.

114. Last night goodbye dinner at S's. Specialty from her southwest region. Confit d'oie, potted goose. Cooked with little cubed potatoes in its own grease. While eating. She regaling company. With stories from land of Oc. Dying language. Spoken by peasant grandparents. Returning daily. From fields. Eating soup at lunch. Soup at supper. One-half glass of red. Poured in remaining broth. In guise of sweet. Grandmother forcefeeding geese. For festive foie gras. Grabbing them secure between legs. Pressing cheeks. *Hop!* Corn's in the gullet. Malheureusement geese capable of ressentiment. So one day S and cousin leaning over grocery wagon. For treats. Exposing cousin's delicious calf between hem and stocking. And *hop!* Goose stretching neck and taking chunk. Cousin still bearing scar.

I asking S to say a few words in Oc. Spoken with old folks. As child.

She acting alternately shocked. Embarrassed.

Leaving Montparnasse apartment. Feeling loved. Warm. Elated. Rain. Crossing 14me in métro. Through train window at

Montparnasse station. Cops chasing platform vendors. Mostly from "the south." Selling peanuts. Silver chains. Lace. Yo-yos lighting up when you toss them. Christmas key season. For sales. Train curving towards Duroc. Thinking cops mean. Watching play of expression on different physiognomies. Notably fat curlyhaired kid. Mouth like Elvis. Expensive sporty dress. Southern American accent. Initially softening authority. In voice. Which authority gathering as speaking. Breathing in deeply. Confident of quality of his humour. Gathering eyebrows and grimacing. Into kind of bullying ugliness. Totally indifferent. To unaesthetic quality of moi chéri. Reflected in métro window.

Blizzard in Bosnia.

### 115. *"STOP SIEGE OF SARAJEVO!"*

Saturday. On pont des Arts. Footpath. Where in movies. Lovers forever sitting embracing. Astride railings. Now a cappella choir. Singing dirges. Light appropriately sepia. Browning huge pinkish dragon two skinny guys inflating. On quay. Below. Banners amassing. STOP SIEGE OF SARAJEVO. AGAINST GREATER SERBIA. AGAINST ETHNIC CLEANSING. More thin men. On stilts. Short fat clowns on ground. With hairless mortuary heads. Large brown coats. Crying. French students in rosy cheeks and long coloured scarves. Moving forward. Chanting. Young guy. Watching from side. Flowing blonde hair. Long khaki raincoat. Huge. Belted and painted a kind of mock camouflage blue and yellow. Feet in old cowboy boots handcut deep into instep. Look in eyes of incredible pain and hardness. "One" imagining. He from Sarajevo.

But crowd pulling forward. Chanting with relief. Releasing pent-up-but-unmentionable remorse. Accrued in months of watching war. On TV. Turning down Saint-Germain. Huge dragon trailing giant nipples. On ground. Balloon insects with mean pointed stingers. Buzzing in on rollerskates. Recorded sounds of sirens and explosions. I going with flow. Getting off on crowd. Edges evanescing. Into moving portrait. Of all of "us." Synthesis in motion. Involving some inner pulsion. Likely sexual. Then H-the-anarchist appearing. Insisting on finding women's contingent. Stepping out of parade. Walking up and down sidewalk. Faster than marchers. But only one older feminist. Distributing pamphlets. Against rape. As weapon of war.

Floating mood broken. Feeling disappointed. I proposing coffee in nice café. Near Odéon.

116. One week left. Slanted place de la Contrescarpe. Sparse trees now leafless. Drunks in sleeping bags. Still waiting for Godot. Leaning buildings. Very old painted sign over charcuterie: AU NÈGRE JOYEUX. In nice inversion—Caucasion (albeit woman) serving. African at table. Rain pelting on it. Face and eyes swollen with cold. Hurrying down narrow market rue Mouffetard. I at first thinking named after exotic warrior sect. From somewhere. It turning out to be named after mouffette, skunk. Due to ubiquitous odour of produce. Street so narrow. Shoulders brushing suspended fur and feathers. Pheasants. Partridges. Rabbits. Cheeses.

Rushing—I straining to grasp this *something* of Paris. Needing to keep inside. Something re *the feeling* of thinking. For—being narrator requiring being "someone." Yet porous (unbounded). Neither excluding. Nor caricaturally "absorbing." Stepping up street. Toward cinema. For film by Perec. Oulipo at last. Granted—dépassé '70s avant-garde (playfully resentful). Unfortunately progress up street. Abruptly prevented. By crowd in peaked caps and scarves. Gathering round man playing accordion. Ballads. Two-steps they dancing at all night guinguettes. Piaf. "La Vie en Rose." Or "La Goualante de pauvre Jean," "Poor People of Paris." People singing hearts out. Collars up. Vaguely elated. No carols. Thank god. I turning right into cinema. But Perec's been replaced. With cartoons for schoolchildren. Now on vacation. Woman at guichet quite apologetic. Perhaps we making error. Reprise in January. I in dismay. Too late for me.

Back up Mouffetard. Stopping to warm in café on high side of Contrescarpe. Owner entering with wreath. I polishing off coffee. Hot. Strong. Certainly delicious. Though sinuses so stuffed—

not tasting a thing. Peeing in Turkish toilet. Spotless. Walking out in rain. Turning home to dry feet. Nurse cold. No use trying to see thirty-eight spectacles. Forty-nine museums. When only six days left.

In studio again. Falling asleep. Dreaming male québécois writer. Plus Pierre-Yves his lover. On canapé. When there coming some word about substantial drop in funding. Meaning end of studio. The guys' ample forms wrapped up in black-and-white sheets. Sobbing. Drinking whiskey. Can't remember rest. Waking. Wanting sex.

117. Grieving cold. Not tasting morsel of fabulous Christmas dinner. R's lover preparing. Foie gras truffé. Sole meunière. Barbary orange duck. Christmas bûche or log. From chez Dalloyau. Best chocolate in Paris. *Plus Z!* Appearing unexpectedly. From visiting young Marxist filmmakers. In suburbs. She meeting at festival chez nous. Now we sitting opposite. In Les Deux Mogots café. She looking unbelievably lovely. Hair pulled back. Wisps around full cheeks. Incredible skin with few well-placed beauty marks. One above her lip. Reading. While I eyeing two Parisians. Could be female couple. Jet black hair. White white skin. Red red lips so frequent here. Completely dressed in black. Air of recklessness. Gazing at horizon in each other's eyes. The Paris I missing. But—twenty-seven francs for tea! Walls butter yellow. Mirrors framed with corrugated marble. Lovely shell pattern in mosaics on floor. Mercifully free. Of canned American music. One hearing increasingly. In cafés. Back out on street. Two cops hanging out. On Saint-Germain-des-Prés. Noticing Z's ragged sheepskin coat. Following us a little. Don't make eye contact. I whispering. Notwithstanding Dunquerque stamp in passport. She smiling mockingly.

118. Waking. Worrying about mortality. Not incongruously Z and I heading out to cimitière Montparnasse. Pausing at dadaist Tzara's grave. Simple block surrounded by fake roses. Then de Beauvoir and Sartre. Under reasonable grey marble. Fruitless search for Man

Ray. But old woman vigorously scrubbing tombstone. Crying out to us. Oh you're looking for Baudelaire. Pointing to weathered monument. Inscribed *General Aupick's family, Ch. Baudelaire, his stepson.* Covered with lilies. Sunflowers. Decaying roses. And poem in glass frame. *Ta tombe est mon alcove,* your tomb is my alcove. Frame also including—wet métro ticket. Stone that moving most. Flat with cast body of young man lying face down on top. One foot literally disappearing into grave. I thinking AIDS. Inscription: *André Y, 1942-90.* And inscribed under that: *Vincent W, 1940-____.*

Z hurrying on. I watching us from distance. Distance of little Paris bubble. Plus something else. Ominous. Her beauty. Decked out in current poverty of youth. Worn boots. Secondhand clothing. Passing single yellow rose (live). On Beckett. Then ludicrously high pedestal. With romantic poet Edgar Quinet's bust perched upon it. Behind walled street and square. Named after him. We now crossing. In café ordering wine. Bread. Sausage. Waiter failing to notice Z's beauty. As if all girls in Paris. Equally sublime.

119. Place de la Bastille. Cavernous café full of young workers. On Christmas break. Short leather jackets. Gauloises. Listening to philosopher. In corner. Cars racing in usual circles. Small shadows mingling with taller shadow of monument in middle. Conjuring huge elephant formerly standing there. Which elephant in reality. Giant maquette for fountain. Never built. Its empty form becoming nest for hundreds of rats. Wherein Hugo's homeless Gavroche taking shelter. Rodents. Soon eating his cat.

Waiter bringing hot chocolate. Creamy. Very dark pure chocolate streaks. Floating on surface. Licking discreetly. Alone. Z having returned chez nous. Saying Paris all right. But hinting my hairdo too smooth. Overly polished shoes. She definitely signing up for work group to Cuba. Deeply I inhaling. Mood-lifting chocolate. Still breathless. From fleeing angry shopkeeper. Having accidentally sullied tight ribbed sweater. While trying on in changing room. With foundation make-up. I applying daily. Since Z perceiving enlarged pores on nose. In light of métro. Dodging down Roquette. Spying running kohl and rouge. In outer boutique mirror. After swearing to vendor I wearing hardly any. Now sipping chocolate-y chocolate. Feeling *No Guilt*. Like French hero(ine) in S's favourite novel. Likewise feeling *No Guilt*. When African lover suiciding. Over French lover's apparent indifference.

Leaving café in cold snowy rain. Strolling. Not noun. But not verb either. I.e. neither excluding. Nor caricaturally absorbing other. Into vortex of vision. But how maintaining one's faith in mark as artist. If not *SomeOne*. I wondering. Strolling past reflection in wine-store mirror. Very short lashes. Also slightly sloppy.

Snowing in Bosnia.


120. Last day. Angry pink-grey dawn. Visible down curved white rue de Grenelle. Over lovely asymmetrical steeples of Saint-Sulpice. Going out to baker's—tempted to run over. But pot of tea waiting. Drastic headache. Coffee withdrawal. Now cultivating eczema. Bags under eyes. With quantities of tea.

One-half hour later. Sky teal blue. Traffic. Shutters up. Curtains grey with soot. Slicing into fresh pain de campagne. Trying to remember quality of smells. From cheese shop. To take along. "Forever."

Last night last supper in café Saint-Germain. "Final" looking out over boxes of geraniums. Steak/frites once more. Allowing self to cry. (No one seeing.) Some ancient sadness pulling back on one. Crying about future. About human condition. Bosnia. French people getting flooded out. Rivers everywhere overflowing banks. Swollen Seine covering the quays. Hoping it rising enough to prevent crossing to right bank. On way to Roissy airport. Then remembering plane leaving from Orly. On south bank. Where I living. Ancient sadness pulling. Until—thanks to carbohydrate loading—laughing.

Late afternoon. Having made last-day discovery—new second-floor café. On Saint-Sulpice. Great view of square. Everything in movement. Pigeons. Branches. Water in fountain. Or—wind falling—hesitating at cusp. Of change. In direction. Which pause I loving. Back along overpriced Grenelle. Shopping for wardrobe. For returning home chic. But buying only lightbulbs. This I finding amusing.

"Home." In driving wind and rain. For meeting with leisure lottery representative. Having cleaned bathroom. Kitchen. Until all sparkling white. Not yet vacuuming living room. When thin well-dressed man. Outdoor Alpine look. Arriving to inspect. Failing even to glance at gleaming scrubbed tiles. Sitting on edge of canapé. By dirty rug. Drinking only half the coffee offered. Then asking—is vacuum cleaner broken.

Walking once more down boulevard Raspail. Past men's clothing-store display. In right display window—male hand rising. From pile of bunched-up coloured papers. Perfect sleeve of perfect coat. Holding tiny clock. While headless standing man in window to left. In dark pants. Shirred purple velvet vest. Pointing towards diminutive timepiece. In hand. Of window on right.


Ready. Washed. Pressed. Smooth. Polished. Having lived in Paris. Then ballpoint bursting from cabin pressure. In plane. All over red jeans. Landing in snowstorm chez nous. Little trucks bustling back and forth over icy surfaces. Russian officers stepping off Aeroflot plane. Saluting someone. Small darkhaired moustached men with glasses. Reading passports quickly. It being New Year's Eve and they wanting to go home. Nervous American girl in French cloche and shoes. Smiling too broadly at customs officer. As if doing something wrong. Then—time being what it is—I trudging in snow down rue-Saint-Denis. Montréal. Québec. Dark Paris outfit and smooth hairdo. Overdressed for here. Where loose bright thick sweaters. Made of hemp. Trope for environmental sensitivity. Appearing under coats. Entering café. Moderately good coffee. Some young architects. Talking of career opportunities. You have to find a place just recovering from war saying one. Get involved in reconstruction.

Bosnia.

"Le Sexe de l'art"

New Year's: 199_

——Over dark overcrowded square——Notre-Dame in lacunae
of fog curtain——Imposing only certain tropes of great beastly
spirit——Corks popping. On curves of bridges. Looking toward
(fog-erased) Grand Palais. At bend of river——Champagne——
Boîtes vibrating Satchmo. C'est si bon——A cliché. She beside me
saying. Very pink lips. Initially not wanting to come. Preferring
riding horses——Still what orgasms angels popping up. Mid walls.
Near Louvre's small eyes. Looking in. Or out. She asking——

——Still in mist——Seeing almost nothing——Past Palais-Royal
gate——Voices of young women drinking rosé. At folded table.
Glasses raised. Fingerless gloves. Reading Colette aloud. In hom-
age. Yellowed pages. Drifting. Past display window. Rue Saint-
Honoré. Lit by Max Ernst reel. Announcing *Le Sexe de l'art*. At
Beaubourg. Two pretty women. Jerky film. "Arousing" each other.
Furtive embarrassed fingers. Entering folds. While giggling into
camera. Then forcing dildo in——Next window. Urinoir. Caption
*The air of Paris*——Next. Catalogue. Opened. At painted opened
legs. Lovely furry snatch. Called *L'Origine du monde*——

——Drifting——Phenomenal unseen racket——S'il vous plaît madame. Les Champs-Elysées——Through hole in mist Molière leaning forward. On seat. Toward Richelieu's street——Right on
Chabanais——Women's bar. Still bright as daffodils. Victory-wing
collars. Poodles. Deep kissing. As before. Drinks likewise

unaffordable. Given dollars. With foreign queen on them——Re-treating. Borrowed room. Two flights up. Over second inner court-yard——How many ~~orgasms~~ hours later. Pulling aside lace cur-tain. Wiping humidity off window——Below. Yet another court-yard. Glass hexagonal roof. Filthy diaper. Lodged in corner of it——

——The room: banal——But finest linen sheets. Saggy chandelier offering special pink light. Adjustable to good degree of skintone——What shadows. Under breasts. Over inner court roof. With dirty diaper on it. Court imposing. On sleep——Pink lips. Waiting in passage. Leading to one more court or opening. Men crowding in. It being courtyard of Godard's *Vivre sa vie*——Di-lapidated pissoir. She having applied. For *poste* of prostitute. Be-ing particularly suited. Hair easily pushed back in place——Stand-ing waiting. In funny inner court. When man of crowd coming up. Saying I want you to get your thing out of here. She saying the only thing I having. Is dollars. With foreign queen on them——

——What ~~orgasms~~ desire to be alone. Pink lips asleep. And smil-ing——Stepping out. Crossing second inner court. Closed union headquarters. Moustached man waiting——Past misty double doors. Likely leading to glass-roofed picture-framing factory. Lodg-ing diaper over——Through winter market. Smell of fragrant quiche. Salty chunks of ham in it. Red lettuce. Screeching. Sound of garbage. Being collected. By Caucasians with degrees——Bump-ing men from "south." S saying. In ciné-café. Sunken armchair. On cold cement. Drinking tea. Reading *Le Monde*——New Tavernier film discussing need for revival. Of French solidarities——I point-ing out. Article declaring work bold in form. No longer finding audience. S shrugging. That old malaise. Between us——

——Drifting——Over Montparnasse. Bar of open oysters. Lips hanging out. Over Diaghilev tiles. Half-eyes in angles. Fat tea-drink-ing Russian——Sitting naturellement by window——On sidewalk. Faint row of motorcycles. Black helmets attached. Crushed roses on cement. Prefiguring death——Ordering carafe——Ambience so damp. Ordering another——Virile-looking greyhaired philosopher type. Behind. Loudly proclaiming. Speed is where it's at. Face very red——Slender acolyte. Lighting cigarettes——Acceleration. Philosopher obsessing. Velocity. I who drive a sports model. Noticing how new construction materials. Making of buildings moving screens. The 21st. Era of nomads: the poor——The rich. More and more. Staying put——

——Mist——Drifting back——Smell of smoke. Crossing Sèvres-Babylone——Ghosts of ceaseless winter demonstrations——Passing men's shop. Opposite old leisure lottery studio. What to my astonishment. But woman's dress now standing. By elegant sleeve. Of capitalist escroc. Where only men's suits before. Latter's hand. Cut off. Dress. Black. Lacy. Calf-length. "One" can wear forever. Making "one" Parisian——Down Grenelle. Cube faces of expensive phantasmagoria. Appearing intermittently in fog——Silk slit of skirt——Ivory trunk——Leopard shade——Droopy eye of pleasure-seeking Frenchman——Sound of child coughing——Voice saying Japonaiseries. C'est normal——Splash of washing streets. So Paris looking clean——Where filth going——Ça m'ennerve, unnerves me. Another voice complaining——

——Drifting——Back over second inner court. Moustached man. Still waiting. Cheap attaché case. By doors of union headquarters. Excuse me. In accent of immigrant. Have you seen the union bosses. Have you seen the militants——She with pink lips. Awake and waiting. Courtesan Liane de Pougy's life. In hand——Having *orgasms* forgotten quiche. Into street again——Luxembourg in fog. Din. Somewhere in background——She saying de Pougy complaining. American lover Nathalie Barney. Lacking in realism. Re: tasks of courtesan——Fog lifting——Tops of passing boots. Iron toes approaching. Delicate hands and cheekbones. H-the-anarchist! Boots she laughing. À la mode. Again. Given transportation strikes—— Accompanying us a little——Loose bomber jackets. Occasionally appearing. Large. For layering sweaters under. Useful on picket lines——Also. On Raspail. Anorexic silhouettes. Of femmes-postiche, ornamental women——

——Raspail. Again——Mist up to shins. Pink lips haletant, breathless. Saying air of Paris. Suffocating her——Small van. Crowding us on sidewalk——Saying tallness. Making her feel like cowboy—— I'll take her to see cowboys. With tight flyless overalls. Showing off balls. Little kerchiefs. Waiting table. Near wax museum——Real cowboys'd kill 'em. She laughing——Instead. Down Odessa—— Fog shifting boundaries——Café at Edgar-Quinet. Having taken on aspect of cabin. Heavy wood. Hotdog stand in corner. But still on menu. Petit salé aux lentils, salt pork with lentils. In garlic butter. Espresso in little cups. Alas. Sugar cubes having given way. To envelopes of granular. So not finishing off. With ritual of browning cube in coffee. Sucking. Sucking——*Duck*. French calling it——

——The room: what juicy ~~orgasms~~ oranges. From market. Sleeping. Waking with chocolate——At Bastille. Mist above knees. Cars racing. Round Revolutionary monument. Where 100,000 socialists. Strewing roses. In memoriam of president. Simultaneously smirking he having two families. Gorgeous veiled mistress. And daughter. Appearing at funeral. Femme légitime, legitimate wife also très chic. I.e. accepting——Caricature of rightist politician. Saying to spouse. Me too I want two wives at funeral. Spouse replying you make me laugh. With your socialist ideas——Pink lips. On boulevard Beaumarchais. Tired of femmes légitimes. Wanting girls like us. Then stepping in dogshit——Oh! she declaring. But it's French dogshit. So artfully arranged on sidewalk. So perfumed——

——Freezing mist. Molecules. Popping in air——Over little park. Entering Cirque d'Hiver——Turquoise pinnacle. Balloons tumbling from crystal-bowl chandeliers. Golden horses. Clearing doorframes——On high trapeze. Four female twisting sculptures.

Lying on each other. Entangled——In ring. Mongolian super-femme. Plus space frog. With breasts. Doing love dance on mushrooms—— Queeny Russian clowns. Entangled. In gowns——Pink lips stage-whispering. In Paris girls like us in freak shows——Terrifyingly skinny French juggler——Air of Paris. Crystal——Métro mouthing din. Of angry youth. Amassing on platforms——African-French child. Pointing. Saying belle. For Africans. Pou-belle, garbage. For whites——Chef des clochards. Loose blanket. Sandals. Rrose Sélavy hat. Begging louder——

——The room: man with briefcase. Still waiting. Outside union headquarters——Pink lips walking about. Touching things elatedly. Having booked for continuous lesbian erotic show. From midnight til dawn. Her way. Of taking Paris. Otherwise. Preferring horses——I stepping out for porto——Drifting. In din —— Suspended frost-flaked foreground. Billboard with twenty little squares. Tight-jeaned prick. In each. Packed in. In as many different ways——Drifting——White truck on sidewalk. Official jumping out. Photographing homeless person. Now requiring ID. Sinon. Prison——Left on Raspail——Across second inner courtyard. Up two flights of stairs. Pink lips waiting. Fine cowboy boots. Tight pants. Silver belt. Silk shirt. Reading in guidebook. Club we going to. Frequented early century. By Barnes & Co.——

——Drifting. Rue du Dragon. Few people. Damp flakes. Guy darkly handsome. Good coat and haircut. Cigarette on lip. Glancing—— Pot-au-feu in wine bar. Deliciously concocted. Re-heated. To lukewarm. In microwave——Drifting——Widely spaced snowflakes. Traffic. As if sleeping——Over Montparnasse——Red steel door with peephole——Guy opening a crack. Demanding money. Opening blind hatch. Into all-red room. Stage two feet from seats. Verging on empty. German dykes on sofa to left. French girls on right. Each with waitress. Dressed as Mädchen In Uniform. Trying to peddle drinks——Waiting——German pair leaving——Waiting. French non-nonplussed——Waiting——Door *at last* bursting open.

Blonde bursting in. Racing to washroom——Stage lighting up——
Blonde strutting out. Nice evening gown. Hair badly combed.
Embarrassed look on face. Doing it for women. Fastest strip in
history. Off with the gloves. Gown. Turning. Bending one second.
To show us her clasp. Fleeing——Then——Rien——

——Drifting——Ultra-ironic smile. On Pink-lips' face——Crumpled
paper. From some fête. Or demo——Van braking on sidewalk.
Nearly hitting us. Wiry guy jumping out. Cellular in hand. Map.
Cigarette. Calculator. Tremendous nervous gestures. Though middle
of night. Unions saying. Entrepreneurial tirelessness. Putting salariat,
working class in danger——Over inner courtyard——No time for
sleep. It being dawn. No time for strolling out again——Cleaning
filthy toilet. Shoving table back under chandelier. Stripping bed of
silky sheets. Still what ~~orgasms~~ embraces——See. I saying to her.
Sitting graciously in armchair. Pulling on her cowboy boots——

——Sauntering——Silent——Sky. Smoky blue——Black bird silhouettes. Above chaos of chimneys——Luxembourg empty. Except. White-painted guy. Dancing along pathetic low railing. Inches
off ground. As if on highwire tightrope. Toeing to left. Toeing to
right. Bowing hopefully. To no one——Out into street——Dogcatcher truck. Buses——Taxi. Cruising past Odéon columns. Actors fasting. For Sarajevo——Leaving enclave. Dissatisfied——Suburbs——Cement saucer of airport——That dogcatcher truck. Pulling up behind. Woman stepping out. White ruff collar. Dark blouse.
Skirt. Very high forehead. Saying I come from war. And here is con-
fusion. Handing out pamphlet. Saying les Bosniennes, Bosnian
women. Saving culture. In chaos. With 100 small attentions. Presenting selves impeccably. Best food. In worst situations——Pink
lips ahead. Smiling. Pointed boots forward. Towards boarding
gate——I turning. Once. Looking——

# Acknowledgements

THIS NOVEL IS IN PART A CONVERSATION WITH SEVERAL OF THE GREAT writers who left their mark on Paris (and on whom Paris left its mark) in the 19th and 20th centuries. These include Honoré de Balzac (especially for his androgynous *The Girl With Golden Eyes*), Gertrude Stein (for her well known opinions on sentences, verbs, the French, Americans, and notions of republic), Charles Baudelaire, Colette, Victor Hugo and his daughter Adèle. In particular, the narrator/author holds a critical dialogue with the ghost of Walter Benjamin regarding his montage method of recounting history. The citations credited to "B" are my often loose translations of his citations of 19th- and early 20th-century authors, as well as paraphrasing and very occasional quoting of his own words from the French version of his famous *Passagenwerk,* translated from the German by Jean Lacoste and published as *Paris, Capitale du XIX$^e$ siècle* (Paris: Les Editions du Cerf, 1989).

I wish to thank the people at Dalkey Archive Press, notably editor Martin Riker, and Chad W. Post, for their excellent work. Thanks also to Mercury Press in Toronto for publishing the Canadian edition of *My Paris* (Toronto: April, 1999).

A special thanks to Dianne Chisholm for superb critical reading and great conversation. And to Carla Harryman, Fred Wah and Robbie Schwartzwald for insightful comments and support.

I am grateful to Helen Mirra for the perfect cover, to Marik Boudreau for the inside photo, and to Traude Bührmann for letting me use the passage cited in section 56 from her novel *Flüge über Moabiter Mauern* (Berlin: Orlanda Frauenverlag, 1987).

And last but of utmost importance, thanks to Anna Isacsson, Sean Holland, Suzette Triton, Nell Tenhaaf, Jacqueline Dumas, Penelope Fletcher-le Masson, Bruce Russell and Nathalie Kermoal.

# LANNAN SELECTIONS

The Lannan Foundation, located in Santa Fe, New Mexico, is a family foundation whose funding focuses on special cultural projects and ideas which promote and protect cultural freedom, diversity, and creativity.

The literary aspect of Lannan's cultural program supports the creation and presentation of exceptional English-language literature and develops a wider audience for poetry, fiction, and nonfiction.

Since 1990, the Lannan Foundation has supported Dalkey Archive Press projects in a variety of ways, including monetary support for authors, audience development programs, and direct funding for the publication of the Press's books.

In the year 2000, the Lannan Selections Series was established to promote both organizations' commitment to the highest expressions of literary creativity. The Foundation supports the publication of this series of books each year, and works closely with the Press to ensure that these books will reach as many readers as possible and achieve a permanent place in literature. Authors whose works have been published as Lannan Selections include: Ishmael Reed, Stanley Elkin, Ann Quin, Nicholas Mosley, William Eastlake, and David Antin, among others.

# SELECTED DALKEY ARCHIVE PAPERBACKS

# FOR A FULL LIST OF PUBLICATIONS, VISIT:
## www.dalkeyarchive.com

# SELECTED DALKEY ARCHIVE PAPERBACKS

# FOR A FULL LIST OF PUBLICATIONS, VISIT:
# www.dalkeyarchive.com